In the sequel to *The Book And The Rose*, it's been several months since Hollywood screenwriter Evans McCoy gave up his life in Los Angeles to move in with his lover, Mio, a retired gay porn star and former high-class rent boy who lives in Barcelona. Their relationship is blossoming, Evans is taking Spanish classes, and is settling in with gusto. Now, he feels love he has never had — not just from Mio, but from the man's entire family. In the back of his mind, however, Evans worries that Mio will tire of him and miss his old life . . .he frets that he will wind up back in L.A. with a loveless existence and a dysfunctional family that doesn't talk and never, ever eats such lavish home-cooked meals like Mama makes.

Sensing his lover's restlessness, Mio fears he doesn't do enough to assure Evans of his commitment. He decides that Evans needs to forget Mio's past once and for all. Since Evans never got to experience the excitement of Mio's hooker world as a client, Mio suggests a sexy trip for two, where he will treat his partner to a decadent, forbidden, roleplaying liaison. He is happy to be Evans's call boy forever, but Evans must go along with everything Mio presents to him.

April Sun in Cuba
Copyright © 2019 A.J. Llewellyn
ISBN: 978-1-4874-2529-6
Cover art by Martine Jardin

Published by eXtasy Books Inc or
Devine Destinies, an imprint of eXtasy Books Inc

Look for us online at:
www.eXtasybooks.com or www.devinedestinies.com

April Sun in Cuba

By

A.J. Llewellyn

DEDICATION

To Mio and Evans who would not let go of me after I wrote The Book and the Rose. This book was a total joy.

Chapter One

Somebody was kissing me. Over and over again, kisses fell like little stars, bright, shiny golden stars from heaven. My lips puckered up for a big one. I heard a chuckle. My lover Mio's lips stopped, raining on my parade, but when I opened my eyes, he was lying right beside me in our bed, smiling.

"You took my kisses away from me." For some reason whenever Mio awoke me that way it reminded me of the gold star system at school. They were my reward. I lived for his kisses. It had been years since I'd been at Lincoln Middle School in Santa Monica, California . . . but I still remembered how excited I got when my teachers gave me gold stars for good behavior. I collected them because for me they were rare. I hadn't been a standout kid. I'd always lingered in the middle of the pack . . . Santa Monica was a long way from Barcelona . . . and so was school. But I still had golden stars.

"Bésame," Mio whispered. "Kiss me." The sun shone on his glistening, astonishingly beautiful body. He laughed so easily these days. I loved the man he'd slowly revealed to me the more time we spent together. I'd once liked his brooding facial expressions, the haunted look in his gaze topped off by his dark, dramatic hair with its widow's peak. Now, I loved his smile, loved each tooth in his magnificent face, the long, slightly irregular lashes lining the most expressive brown eyes I'd ever seen. They were the color of tiger's eye, and I regularly hunted in jewelry stores for cuff links with stones to match them.

I shifted my body closer and kissed him. His mouth met mine in an instantly hot clashing of tongues. He tasted wonderful. How did he manage to taste so sweet in the morning? I had breath like a sick moose and Mio was a tasty pastry. I could smell lavender fabric softener on our one-thousand thread count sheets as my mouth moved past his chin to his throat, then down his chest, lapping at his silky skin.

His breath caught in his throat. My favorite kind of music. It was all I could hear, his quickening breath, as my mouth roved his toned, muscular body.

I focused on the tent he was making in our tousled bed sheet. He stifled a moan as I rubbed my chin against his still-hidden cock. I licked the top of the tent. His hand moved to the back of my neck. He thrust his hips up toward me. I knew what he wanted, but I ignored him, kissing along the sheet's resting place at the delicious curve of his hips and the start of his treasure trail. He'd let it grow back for me. I kissed the dark dusting of hair as his breathing became labored.

Sometimes I couldn't believe that this gorgeous sun god was mine, that he was in my head, my heart, my house . . . that he lived with me and came home to me each night. Well, it wasn't like he had a regular job or anything, but sometimes, just sometimes, when he went to the gym, or a meeting, or even to grab coffee with one of his friends on the Ramblas, I worried, terribly, that he wouldn't come back. Nothing in his manner or in our interactions with one another gave me any reason to feel so insecure.

Mio-Alejo Cortez, however, was a recently retired rent boy, long-retired gay porn star, but still a popular celebrity in his hometown of Barcelona. I'd had no idea who he was when we'd met on a business trip in London. We'd made eye contact, had some mighty fine sex for two days and the bastard took my soul home with him in his deluxe baggage,

2

along with the little bottles of shampoo courtesy of the hotel.

And now . . . long after his truth had been revealed and Mio gave up his decadent, lucrative lifestyle for me, we were happy. Oh, so happy. We sometimes argued about whether it was appropriate to accept gifts from his former clients, but the truth was, he liked the stuff they gave him. Now that he was no longer putting out, however, the gifts had tapered off. One man in particular still sent Mio lavish candies and packages of rare coffee and tea. Somehow, Mio had convinced me it was okay to —

"Mio." I sat up on the bed.

He looked alarmed. "You're going to stop now, Evans? Are you serious?"

"I just figured out why you taste so good."

His angst turned to cat-like satisfaction. "You caught me."

He'd been eating *marrons glacés*, which until I'd met Mio, I'd never even heard of, much less tasted. They were the most delicious things ever. Candied chestnuts that were prepared with sugar and syrup and . . . cost a bomb.

Reaching down to the box I realized was sitting on the floor beside our bed, he plucked one out and fed it to me with his fingers. That was another thing. He had a sweet tooth and ate stuff like this all day long but still maintained a gorgeous, fat-free physique. Me, one marrons glacés and I'd have to run a mile or else my belly would show its inclination to reveal its inner lard-ass.

God, it was good. Mio grinned, watching me chew. He leaned up and kissed me. But I was no fool. He wanted my sloppy seconds. His sudden movement made the sheet slip.

"Oh-oh," he said as his cock sprang into view. The leaking head bore my favorite tell-tale signs of Mio's arousal. "Now you've done it. You see what you do to me?" Mio's playful tone, his heavily accented, but very good English all served to further inflame my desire for him. I bent to take

3

that thick, wonderful cock into my mouth. He let out a loud, "Yessss!"

I loved the taste of his salty cock mingling with the sugary syrup.

"Good?" he asked, his eyes becoming heavy-lidded.

I came off him for a moment to say, "Very good. I would like to brand this as a new food group. Cock glacés."

He gave me a slow, seductive smile, reaching down again to the wooden box. He dipped his fingers into a pink paper cup, then lifted it to the bed as he began smearing his cock with syrup and spices. The cinnamon swirl sliding down his shaft fell against my tongue. I licked and sucked at Mio as he kept piling on the sauce. I'd have to run six miles to work off this early morning treat.

Mio lay back as I pushed the sheet off him entirely. I knelt between his honey-colored thighs and began working on him in earnest. I sometimes had to force myself not to think about his previous lovers... Mio loved me. Not them. I made him happy... God, I hoped I made him happy...

His hips rocked upward to meet every pull of my hungry lips. I loved sucking and licking him at the same time because I knew how much he liked it. What separated me from the men Mio had dated and the ones he'd serviced was that he spent so much time figuring out what they wanted, whereas I spent every waking moment learning what he wanted.

Mio had the perfect cock. It was big and thick and always got hard for me. My lips reached the base of his cock, and I breathed in through my nose. Breathing was everything when one had a gigantor like this to nurse.

I sucked him back to the top of the head, my lips remaining tight around the crown. I let my mouth slide back down. He arched up, anxious as ever for full immersion. His cock tasted so good, syrupy good, and I released him for one more moment to share the flavor with him.

He wasn't pleased.

Mio accepted my kisses and clearly enjoyed the taste of cock glacés, but he wanted me to keep sucking his cock.

Gladly.

I went back to work, loving the task ahead of me. I let go of his rigid shaft again to suck his balls, but he liked that. His hand was back on my head, stroking my hair. I could almost hear him thinking, Good boy.

Mio's need became urgent when I returned to his cock. I wanted to lick his ass, but there was no time. He floundered against the sheets as if he couldn't take a second more. I put my mouth right back on him, Mio nudging his way back where he belonged. I'd sucked away most of the syrup, and all I had left now was him. Not that I wanted anything else.

It was all about him. I fondled his balls, holding them tightly in my right hand as I began sucking harder, taking him deeper into my mouth again. Mio's legs fell open, his body reacting to me the way I loved it to do. He fucked my face, his head tossing back and forth.

"Evans . . . Evans . . . Evans . . ."

He was coming. With my left hand I stroked his ass cheeks, the thing he loved most when I was sucking him. His secret, tender spot was the crease in his cheeks, and he almost flew off the bed as I brushed my fingertips against them.

"Quiero . . ." He started saying, I want . . . but he didn't finish the sentence. His hand gripped the back of my neck, his fingers stroking it. I felt his hot gaze on my face but concentrated on sucking him up and down, longer, tighter, saltier . . . and then he came. The rupture was deep and powerful.

On camera, he'd been a known and prolific gusher. In private, it was the same. He came hard, and his cream was thick, juicy and very, very white. I swallowed his load but couldn't quite take it all. He reached for me, licking my mouth as I came up to his face, telling me he loved me as he sucked on my lips and tongue.

"Quiero follarte," he said, his words a moan. "I want to fuck you."

I bent to lick the shaft again, cleaning his cock head. He smiled lazily, reaching for me again. He pulled me into his arms, giving me his fingers to suck. Syrup still stuck to them. Lucky syrup.

He began kissing me. Apart from being the best lover I'd ever had, he was an amazing kisser. He turned me onto my back, lying right up against me, his fingers suddenly probing my mouth. It was one of the funniest, oddest yet most erotic habits of Mio's. He liked reaching for my tongue. He licked it, his own tongue moving across my lips, then back into my mouth again. He could do this for hours, prepare me for his cock with long kisses, teasing fingers and —

The phone beside our bed rang. We smiled at each other. Only a handful of people had the number. It would either be his mother, his sister, Belen, or one of her two kids. We loved little Violetta and Primo as if they were our own.

Mio's indulgent expression shifted into something else . . . a predatory gleam infiltrated his features as he sat up, rigid.

"Cristóbal."

I hunted through my memory banks for which one was Cristóbal. A former co-worker from the rent boy game . . . or was he a former lover?

Mio grinned into the phone. A former client. He must have been a good one An occasional few still called. I could hear a man's deep voice rumbling as he spoke, but couldn't make out his words. Why did this asshole have our private number? Mio, who couldn't bear to see another man even glancing in my direction, was laughing now. At another man's early morning chatter. I rose from the bed. He didn't try to stop me. He began to pace naked in the sunny room. I'd hoped to linger in bed with him, but not when Cristóbal was making my lover smile that way.

I threw on some shorts even as I caught Mio's tsking sound and the vehement shaking of his head.

Too bad. He wanted me naked. I wanted him to myself. I left the room, trying to keep my pace casual, unaffected. I should have been an actor instead of a screenwriter and producer. What I really wanted to do was rip the phone out of the wall, then find Cristóbal and stomp all over him. People like him called Mio for one thing.

They wanted him to fuck them.

In the kitchen, I took the coffee from the freezer. Another gift from Mio's admirer. I eyed the wall clock. Belen and the kids would be coming for breakfast in an hour. I opened the bag and inhaled the fragrance of the Kopi Luwak, which has the distinction of being the world's most expensive coffee at around a hundred and sixty dollars a pound.

I glanced across the expanse of hardwood floor separating me from Mio. He was still pacing. I could hear the words, mi marido, my husband. There were still a few . . . malingerers from Mio's former life who didn't know he'd quit the business. When they did resurface with offers of outlandish getaways he used to live for and vast sums of money that were the norm for him, he never hesitated telling them he was no longer on the game. His old life had given him the taste for the finer things such as the Indonesian coffee in my hands. He missed the food more than anything, so I encouraged him to shop online.

Some of the men became hysterical, and Mio would placate them, steering them toward other porn-starring rent boys. His fierce movements told me he was a little agitated. This guy was probably not taking no very well.

7

Mio mentioned the name Marcus. His closest gay friends, Jaime and Marcus, rented themselves out as a couple. Mio funneled a lot of business toward them with encouraging words for his former clients, "You'll get two for the price of one."

Yeah. True. But I knew that no two guys were any match for one Mio.

That was the problem. Mio was no used-up shell of a gay porn star. He wasn't a vacuous, soulless pin-up boy wasted on steroids and obsessed with gym workouts. Many of the performers I'd met through Mio had serious substance abuse issues and a history of sexual abuse, astonishing tales of childhood trauma that led to them to going on the game. Some were so blasted each time we saw them that I worried about them when we said goodbye.

But not Mio. He had drifted into hustler sex because he had a high sex drive and enjoyed the lifestyle and the attention. By the time I'd met him he'd quit doing porn but had a lucrative callboy business. Now that had fallen by the wayside, too. He'd reinvented himself as a model, sometime actor, and together we had produced a movie and now had a gay Spanish soap opera on TV in Barcelona.

It was a smash hit.

Women and men loved Mio. He loved them back. All of them. He was one of the few sex performers who'd crossed the invisible lake and made a success of it. He had oceans of gold stars to his credit. I was certain he was happy, and he'd willingly told people to stop calling his private line. He'd changed his cell phone number and shredded his old contact files filled with minute details of what his clients liked.

I used to obsess over those. He'd started one on me, too. Not because I was his client but because with so many men in his life, he had to keep our preferences straight . . . as it were. I spooned five tablespoons of coffee into the pot.

"Tesoro." Treasure? He was calling Cristóbal his treasure? Startled, I glanced up from the coffee maker to see Mio watching me from the kitchen door. Why did I always think the worst? Why did I worry?

Then I remembered it had been just nine months since I'd given up my life in Hollywood, California, to be Mio's life partner in a city I was still learning, and immersing myself into a culture and language that were still strange to me. We'd met almost a year ago, and everything about our relationship had been fast. Sometimes I still reeled when I thought about how quickly Mio had convinced me he wanted this . . . wanted me.

He had thrown on jeans and a T-shirt. I gave him a sunny smile. He instantly relaxed and moved closer to give me a kiss. "I go get us some pastries. Don't drink all the coffee without me, guapo."

"I won't," I promised. He grabbed his wallet and left the apartment. I slumped against the kitchen counter. I had to get over this terrible insecurity. My incredibly nutty sister, the actress Nora North, had come out of rehab, found her lost marbles, reinvented herself as a TV talk show guru in LA and offered me some sage advice. I reminded myself of it often.

"Mio loves you. He loves how normal you are. He fell for you knowing you had no idea who he was. He loves your confidence. Never act anything but serene around him."

Truly, it had become my mantra.

It was probably the sanest thing she'd ever said in her whole life, and I was glad she had. In my darkest moments, I doubted her and reminded myself she was a serious loon, but I knew in my heart she was right. Mio hated when I got insecure, and I did my damndest not to show it.

I'd known about his files from my very first visit to Barcelona. I'd gone through his desk when he'd forgotten to lock it one night. I'd uncovered his secret life. Once I knew, he never lied about it, but at first, he was unwilling to quit. For a brief moment, I'd joined him in his vocation, but I couldn't handle it. I'm still glad I did it because I learned a lot about Mio. He's the sort of man who gives a hundred percent to anything he does.

Except finishing what we started in bed this morning . . .

Stop it . . . you are just being a big baby . . .

I sighed. Waiting for the coffee to brew, I checked my voicemail messages as I heard him leave the apartment. I had a Spanish class at two. My teacher was calling to confirm. I couldn't miss another one. Mio frequently got me to play hooky so we could be together, but I suffered for my lapse in judgment at his family's big Sunday lunches where nobody spoke English. Without being able to converse fluently in Spanish, nobody heard me as food bowls flew around the table. Some days I was lucky to land a spoonful of carrots.

My sister had left a text message on my cell phone begging for a part in our soap opera. Not only could she not speak Spanish but she had ruined my career in Hollywood. We'd had the number one sitcom on network TV when she had a meltdown, streaking naked down Ventura Boulevard, brandishing a gun. A lot of therapy and serious rehab all documented on a TV show had helped her, but I didn't trust her.

As for Mio, neither did he. Not after she'd punched me in the face and said terrible things. Addicts are hideous creatures when they are coming off their drugs of choice. No . . . I respected her newfound sobriety and forgave her for what she did to me. But I would never forget.

I deleted her message and got the cups ready on a tray. I sliced up an apple and eyed the wall clock. He'd been gone seven minutes. The bakery was across the road.

Whenever I wanted to act a fool and throw things around, I remembered that Nora considered me normal. I was anything but. Loving Mio had brought out the crazy man in me. Why did love unhinge all my well-oiled good intentions?

The front door opened and closed. Mio was back.

"Quick. Bedroom," he said, running past me. "I think Marcus saw me."

Shit.

I quickly poured the coffee. Somebody was pounding on our front door. Any second now, Marcus would be at the kitchen window. I sloshed milk into my cup, shoved the bottle back into the fridge and bolted to the bedroom with the tray.

"Hello?" Marcus was tapping at the kitchen window as I shut the door on the world.

"Did he see you?" Mio looked concerned.

"I don't think so."

"Good. Now get your clothes off. I want my naked man back."

I handed him the tray. Shucking my shorts, I noticed he had a sprinkling of powdered sugar on his lips.

"You bought Nun's sighs," I said.

He narrowed his eyes. "What is the Spanish name?"

"Suspiros de Monja," I said, without thinking.

"Then you can have one, naked man."

I crawled onto the bed beside him. He put his hand into the paper bag and withdrew one of the golden, crispy mounds.

I could smell candied fruit and almost moaned with pleasure as I bit into it. So soft and gooey on the inside . . . mmm . . . orange peel and powdered sugar on the outside.

He kissed me, anxious for his sloppy seconds. We kissed and ate our way through half a dozen of those sinful treats, swallowing our coffee.

We grinned at each other when we heard Marcus yelling, "I know you're awake. I smell your coffee!" We loved Marcus, but he had no concept of boundaries. Once we opened the door to our favorite stray cat friend, he'd be here all day.

"No more Suspiros de Monja for us," Mio said, peering into the paper bag. "We only have a few left for Belen and the babies."

"Or . . . we can eat these ones and buy them more," I suggested, my hands moving to Mio's body. He grinned at me, but our sultry kisses were interrupted by a honking sound. We both pulled back, staring at one another.

Honk, honk!

"They're early," Mio said, stating the obvious.

"I know they're in there." God. It was Marcus again. We threw on clothes, and I ran to the front door as Mio cleaned up the bedroom and dropped our breakfast remnants into the kitchen sink. Belen stood at the front door, Violetta's hand dangling from her fingertips, and Primo laying a furious hand on the new toy Ferrari I'd bought him for his birthday. I was beginning to regret that particular purchase. He drove into the entrance, right over my foot, giving me the finger, one of Mio's bad habits he'd picked up in his short three years on earth.

Five-year-old Violetta stepped inside, a big, beautiful smile on her face. She was a pint-sized bombshell, a girly girl whose passion for tutus was outmatched only by her love of tiaras. She was wearing both, plus the violet colored T-shirt I'd bought her a few days ago.

"You look gorgeous," I told her. Belen released her daughter to the apartment. I could hear Mio playing noisily with Primo as Belen pushed her sunglasses to the top of her head. Her beautiful eyes, a mirror for Mio's, reflected her anguish. Embroiled in a tough custody battle with her ex-husband, she struggled with being a single mom and budding author. Mio and I were supporting her in every way we could, including financially, but the strain was showing.

"Did you get any sleep?" I asked as she hugged me.

She shook her head.

"You'll have some breakfast, and then you can take a little nap. Mio and I will take the kids out for the day."

"No breakfast for me but the kids, oh yes." She kicked off her shoes and strolled off to the guest room. I was about to shut the door, but Marcus barreled through it. His love, Jaime, was in London, shooting a sex scene for Lucas Entertainment. Actually, he was shooting several scenes back to back, and the company would edit them and release them for whatever projects they had in mind. The two men often shot scenes together, but Jaime had gone on his own to London since Marcus had private clients to service.

"I knew you were home," he said, brushing past me. "I hope you didn't drink all the coffee, Evans."

Why did everybody accuse me of that?

Primo zoomed around the apartment in his candy-apple-red Ferrari, Mio playing cop to Primo's speeding ticket.

"And you're not wearing your seat belt," Mio said, ticking off an imaginary note pad in his hand. Primo laughed, giving his uncle the finger.

"Good boy." Mio nodded.

"Don't tell him that!" Mio exasperated me. Just because he was charming and made cops laugh with that routine, didn't mean Primo could pull it off when he graduated to a real car.

"Hey, Marcus." Mio hugged the other delinquent in our lives. "How was the date last night?"

Marcus knew he had to be careful around the kids.

"Weird," he said. "I've been dying to tell you. "He was one of those guys who likes to wear diapers and get spanked."

Violetta stared up at him. I grabbed her hand and took her to the kitchen with me. She had a little collection of vintage aprons on a hook beside mine. She loved helping me to cook.

"Mama made macaroni again," she said, looking sad. It tore my heart to think of how beautifully Belen and Mio's mom cooked and how Belen thought defrosting frozen mac and cheese every night was suitable fare for her kids.

"Well then, you can have whatever you want for breakfast."

"I want . . ." Her little eyes lit up when she spied the pastry bag. "Those, Evans!"

Reaching for the bag I noticed there were four Nun's sighs left in there. Two each for Violetta and Primo. No. We had Marcus, the other baby, to feed.

"Mio!" As soon as I called his name, my lover was beside me, Primo tossed over his shoulder.

"What do you need, guapo?"

"More of these."

Mio nodded. "I'll take the kids over to the bakery." His voice dropped. "You gotta talk to Marcus. He's upset because Jaime is having an affair with his scene partner. You can make him understand."

He kissed my cheek. "And you're making frittatas, yes?"

Yes, I'd make frittatas. He left the house with the kids in hand. I shot Marcus a look. He was depressed. I poured him coffee and waited. I didn't think I was the right person to counsel him on his partner's behavior. I was still picking my way through some unexploded land mines myself.

I took a dozen eggs out of the fridge and a host of vegetables. Marcus watched me work. He never offered to help because he broke things. I don't mean eggs. I mean things. Marcus was the sweetest guy in the world, but he was a big, clumsy oaf with beefy fingers that always dropped things.

His many hours in the gym were a costly mistake in my opinion. He had a handsome face, dark curly hair and puppy dog eyes, but also an enormously muscular, condom-full-of-walnuts look I didn't find attractive, but a lot of gay men did. His increased bulk only made him a little more . . . ham-fisted, but the man had a heart of gold.

He was American like me and, frankly, he was my saving grace in this town because I longed to speak English sometimes and hang out with somebody who knew what a Ho Ho was. And I don't mean the drunken, slutty boy kind.

"What's going on?" I asked him. He'd hooked up with prolific gay porn star Jaime Jacinto—one of the few performers I knew who worked with his real name—via a long-standing Twitter flirtation. Jaime was from Madrid but had lived all over the world. He and Marcus, a rising porn model and bodybuilder, had hooked up in person, made out in some Barcelona nightclub six months ago and were now joined at the brawny hip.

Marcus and Jaime loved their lifestyle. They did go to amazing places and had once camped for five days in the Sudanese desert, blasting Facebook with their photos. But at this moment, Marcus wasn't looking very happy.

"He did a scene with that Italian model."

"Which Italian model?" I asked. Marcus was under the delusion that I knew all the porn stars on a first-name basis. I knew very few of them. We'd tucked Marcus and Jaime under our wings, and Mio, understanding my need for an American buddy, had encouraged the friendship. Had I been even slightly attracted to Marcus he would have slammed the door on the two men long ago,

"Dino Martino," he said. Man, some of these porn stars gave themselves the stupidest names.

"Isn't he married to another man?"

"Yes, but so what? Brad Pitt left Jennifer Aniston for

Angelina Jolie. Men leave. Especially gay ones."

That was so true I had no smart and snappy comebacks.

I loaded up the casserole dish with the frittata mixture, sprinkling a mixture of cheese on top.

"More," Marcus commanded. "What . . . are you afraid of running out for cripes' sake?"

I got a little more heavy-handed with the cheese, and he grunted his satisfaction.

We didn't have long, so I had to keep his latest counseling session brief. I picked up the dish, he opened the oven door, and I slid the container inside.

"Marcus, what did he tell you exactly?"

"That they did a scene and it was really hot. They snuggled off camera." That was the word he used, Evans. Snuggled."

Oh, lordy. I'd be upset, too. Snuggled suggested an intimacy missing from most gay sexual encounters. Especially ones filmed for the camera.

"Okay. What else?"

"Lucas Entertainment booked a second shoot in some fancy hotel in the south of France for the weekend, and he's going there . . . with Dino."

"Did he invite you?"

"No . . . but he didn't say I couldn't go, either."

"Do you want to go?"

"Yes, but I can't. Jaime booked me solid until he gets back."

I'll just bet he did . . . man . . . I wonder if he was planning this all along . . . I wiped down the kitchen countertops a little more aggressively than I needed to. They weren't cheating on me. It was a fine line in porn partnerships. Most men had an agreement that cheating for film was business. Fooling around when the cameras stopped rolling wasn't acceptable unless the men talked about it first and both partners were on board with it.

"It was hard to say yes, that he could do it, but what could I say? At least he was honest with me."

Big, bad, macho Marcus looked devastated. Underneath the handsome, bulked exterior lurked a sweet and wounded marshmallow heart.

"I love him," he said. "What if Dino takes him away from me?"

"He won't." I could hear the front door opening. "Listen to me, let him have his fun. He'll come back to you. Keep your distance this weekend. Work your jobs. Put some fun posts on Twitter. Make him think you're having the best, most wonderful time this weekend. Make him jealous. Make him feel like he's really missing out not being here."

"Yeah, I like that idea." He straightened, his eyes gleaming at his new game plan. He was happy now, but I was a wreck. I could barely look at my lover, who returned with a couple of pineapples and bags of pastry. He tried to kiss me, but I turned my cheek. I wasn't being fair to Mio, but my heart hurt for Marcus. My heart ached for me . . . for what would happen if Mio's head turned in another man's direction.

I moved away from him and opened the oven door, checking on my frittata. It was a diversion. The frittata was nowhere near ready.

"What's wrong?" Mio asked, but I couldn't explain. I was saved from having to say anything by the kids stampeding into the kitchen in search of food.

CHAPTER TWO

The thing about learning Spanish at the Don Quijote
School in Barcelona was that it was both good and bad.
The school was excellent, but its name was a constant reminder of the most famous mythical son of the city — the fact
that he tilted at romantic windmills wasn't lost on me. Don
Quixote (spelled the traditional way) has been a big part of
my relationship with Mio. We both love the literary charac-
ter and regularly give money to the man portraying him for
the tourists along the Ramblas. A horse-riding knight bearing a sword and roses . . . Mio had once come chasing after
me in LA with roses. He wasn't riding a horse, though. He'd
come in a taxi.

I tried to focus on the class. Really, I did. I had been the
perfect host all morning but insisted on going to my class.
Mio had been disappointed, as were the children. They all
went swimming at the private indoor pool of our apartment
complex without me. A tearful, adorable Primo clung to my
legs, crying hot tears as I left them at the door. I adored that
little boy, and he knew it. It was a hollow victory for me because I found it hard to concentrate. My class of eight was
way ahead of me. I'd missed three sessions and had a hard
time following the conversation running around the oval table in our very modern, hip classroom.

Our teacher, Hilario, was a gem, but sitting there at that
moment was like being at Mio's family table.

Christ . . . we'll be there for Sunday lunch tomorrow. I'll
be lucky if I get a string bean at this rate . . .

Hilario was gifted and patient. He didn't tear at his hair and throw his hands in the air calling us imbécils like my first private teacher had. I worked hard to show interest in the lesson. Inside, my heart was trying to remain whole, trusting. I tried hard not to think about poor Marcus posing for photos, pretending to drive Primo's toy Ferrari. We'd posted the photos online, devising light-hearted captions that hid a darker thought; look cheating lover, breaker of my heart . . . I'm having so much fun without you!

The class session ended as it always did in the immaculate, pebbled courtyard where we had to order our coffees of choice from the kiosk in Spanish. I couldn't remember the word for milk, a simple thing, until Mimi, my new friend from the Bronx, New York whispered, "Leche," in my ear.

"What's the matter with you?" she asked as we squeezed around the only remaining table. "You're all over the place today."

The truth was, I knew that I couldn't live without Mio anymore. I didn't want to live in this world without him. I'd fade away without his love, his face, his tongue on my skin. I'd never felt that way about any man. He had become my whole family because my own was so fucked up. Since I'd discovered I was adopted and Nora North came looking for me, my parents had just about disowned me. They saw it as my just desserts when my sister turned out to be a raving lunatic, and my show got axed.

Mio and his family were all I had. I'd left my life. I stayed in touch with friends, but nobody had the power to destroy my world the way he did.

We had mutually agreed that without each other, Mio and I would die. We were meant to be together. Apart, we might find sanity, like Don Quixote did when he was forced to turn his back on his feelings for Dulcinea, but that was no longer possible for us. Well, for me, certainly. I couldn't return to my old life. It had become clear my father didn't like or respect me anymore. It was still a shock. As for my mother . . . To her, I was the invisible man. I once mentioned this to Nora, who in typical Hollywood fashion, asked me, "Which version? The one with Claude Rains or Chevy Chase?"

I stirred my coffee.

"You'll make butter if you keep going," Mimi warned, and I came back to earth. "Boyfriend trouble?"

"Hell, no. Mio's wonderful. Just worried about a friend." I kept seeing the pain behind Marcus's goofy grin as he mugged for the photos. Was it possible to stop somebody's heartbreak before it happened? I had a bad feeling about Jaime and his liaison with Dino Martino. Why couldn't men buy insurance against their emotions the way they could with their lousy driving?

"You sure?" Mimi asked.

I nodded. We slid into conversational Spanish. Hilario turned to me. "As for you, Señor McCoy, when you are at your boyfriend's family table tomorrow, how will you say, I'd like some turkey please?"

All gazes turned to me. Holy butter bean, Batman.

"Um . . . Me gustaría por favor, un poco de pavo."

Hilario stared at me a moment before nodding his approval. "Very good. And don't forget to speak loudly and don't be afraid to snatch the first plate you see that has something you want. I've had dinner with you and Mio's family. They're like the roller derby. With everyone smoking crack."

I laughed then, the first good belly laugh I'd had that day. He wasn't wrong. I loved Mio's family, but when it came to food, it was every man for himself.

Outside the building, I was surprised to see Mio lounging against a tree waiting for me. He was alone. I loved the light I saw shining in his eyes the moment he saw me. He pushed himself away from his perch and came over to me, his sexy swagger a little off-kilter. He looked at my mouth the way he always did, as if he couldn't wait to possess it. He cupped the back of my head and kissed me.

He tasted of ice cream. And coffee.

Mio greeted Mimi, then took my hand, and we crossed the road. Carrera de Mallorca was a typical Barcelona Street. The traffic was relentless, but due to its European location, it had a plethora of motor scooters, motorbikes, and those tiny, idiotic cars that everyone loved over here but would never survive a week on the average US freeway. Mio held onto me, switching sides as we reached the median strip and crossed the other half of the street.

Advertising pennants promoting the stage show Mama Mia and the upcoming three-day Sónar music concert in June flapped from Streetlamps and telegraph poles. Barcelona was home to many concerts. Mio and I went to them all. He kissed my hand as we reached the other side.

"You're so protective," I said. "I love that about you." It still amazed me how well-mannered he was. He always walked on the outside of a footpath, putting himself in the potential for harm's way when we crossed the street.

"I love you, Evans. Don't you know that by now?"

"Yes. I know it."

He drew me into his arms and kissed me. Thank God Barcelona wasn't shy about man-on-man love.

"Then what am I doing wrong?" he asked when he broke off our dazzling embrace.

"What?"

"You've been upset all day. Guapo . . . you wouldn't kiss me in the kitchen . . ." His voice trailed away, and he began walking in circles. He was really upset now. "Is it . . . was it the phone call from Cristóbal?"

"No . . . yes . . ."

21

"You want me to change the number?"

I looked down the street at the tight maneuvers of the city's scooter riders in a stream of bigger vehicles. Just like them, I had to duck and weave carefully. I didn't want him to think I was the big, bloody basket case that I was.

"The answer must be yes for you to think so long," Mio said. "What am I doing wrong? I've tried so hard—"

"No. I trust you, Mio. It's not you. It's me."

His face turned ashen. "What are you saying?"

"I'm afraid of losing my life with you." Tears pricked my eyes. "I'm sorry. It's not anything you're doing. It's . . . me," I finished lamely.

His whole faced collapsed in relief. I'd had no idea of the tension he must have been feeling.

"Guapo . . ." He took me into his arms and kissed me again. "I thought you wanted to leave," he said against my lips.

"I would die without you." I loved the way his fingers stroked my face. I could feel his hard cock grinding against mine. We were a mile from our house. We wouldn't get far with our bodies in this state.

Mio gently bit my bottom lip.

"What would you like for me to do? What would make you happy? In this moment?" He kissed my eyes, my nose, my mouth, not waiting for an answer.

"Take me home and fuck me."

"I can do that. And then . . . I have a plan."

"What kind of a plan?"

He ignored me, whistling for a taxi. The driver did an illegal U-turn over the grassy median strip. Mio laughed as the black cab with the wide yellow stripes down its side screeched to a halt beside us.

"You think it's safe?" I asked Mio.

"If we die, we do it together," he said. He was right. We

made out all the way home. Mio paid the driver, who smiled his thanks for Mio's huge tip.

"I am a fan," he whispered.

Mio just smiled back. He took constant recognition with good grace. "Did you notice what happened back there?" he asked me as we entered our gated property, crossing the lush, landscaped lawns toward our front door.

"In the taxi?"

"No, Evans. When we talked."

"I don't know what you mean."

He unlocked the front door to our apartment, and the children ran to us. Marcus, who'd been watching over them, wheeled the broken Ferrari toward us. "Sorry, Evans . . . I don't know how I did it, but the wheels came off."

I gazed at Primo. He had taken the disaster in stride. He was such a good-natured little thing—until he got behind the wheel of his car. He gazed up at me, and I knew, just knew he wasn't worried because he knew I'd replace his broken toy.

"Primo, I'll buy you another one," I promised.

"We want another swim," Violetta announced. "With you, Evans."

"We all want to swim with Evans . . . and we'll take you," Mio said. "Now do you notice?" His attention was back on me.

I lifted Primo into my arms. "No. What am I supposed to be noticing?"

"We had this conversation and the last one . . . in Span-ish!" He kissed me, then turned to the children. "Kids . . . we need five minutes. Make me a castle with your blocks, and the best one wins a prize."

"Oh, boy!" Violetta squeaked.

"Yeah!" Marcus said, following her.

Primo tottered after them both, even though his building

skills were minimal. He was more fond of tearing things down with karate chops.

"Marcus is building a castle too." Mio grinned at me. He shoved me toward the bedroom.

He closed and locked the door. That was a necessity since the kids adored barging in on us. He pushed me to the bed. I grinned up at him, but his mood was serious.

"Turn over. On your hands and knees," he commanded.

Man, I was already hard. I did as I was told and he knelt on the bed behind me, running his hands over my ass and thighs. I stared up at Picasso's painting of Don Quixote. For us, the Barcelona literary legend was our relationship god. Don Quixote, believer of dreams, lover of love, tilting at windmills. Once I'd thought long and lasting love with Mio was an impossibility. Now I was on my knees on the bed I shared with him as he rained kisses on my back and ass.

Mio's hands moved under my belly to unsnap my belt. He unfastened the button at the waistband of my pants and lowered the zipper. He'd had practice. He kept kissing my clothed ass as he finally got to work on my pants and boxer briefs. He pushed up my shirttail and kissed my back, his mouth moving along my hips. He placed a long, slow kiss on my tailbone, then began to tongue his way down my crack. He must have known my cock was already hard for him. I was sporting a painful boner before he even reached around to touch it. He moaned into my ass as his tongue began to work furiously at my hole. I arched my butt up, head down as he licked and sucked me. It felt so amazing. He knew how to reach all my dark places, bringing light and pleasure to every last nerve. He leaned back, and I would have gone berserk except that I could hear him unzipping his pants.

Thank God. He reached under the pillow beside me for the chocolate flavored lube we'd bought a few days ago. It was almost empty.

"Just enough," he whispered. "We need more." He kissed my ass cheeks. "A lot more."

He smoothed some onto my ass, and I squirmed in anticipation. Since we'd discovered it in Skorpius, a hot little sex shop along the Gran Via, we had fallen in love with the stuff. Mio had to have a taste, his fingers and tongue dipping into me. At last, he couldn't stand it. He needed more chocolate. He needed me.

Pulling my hips toward him, he entered me, my body welcoming his intrusion. He plunged in and out of me, the smell of chocolate heating up between us. He dipped his fingers between our bodies, holding them to my mouth. I turned my head slightly to lick them, sucking on his index finger as he pounded into me. He hunkered down to give me his mouth. Our tongues danced over one another. He picked up the pace, slamming in and out of me. Every time he pulled out, I begged.

"Please."

He taunted me with his cock, taking it away, then giving it back to me. I arched up to him, trying to keep him in me. When his arm curled up under my belly, pulling me tightly against him, I knew he was close. With his free hand he stroked my cock, his body melded to mine. He came hard, my own eruption seconds away from his. He came so deeply inside me, I could feel every thrust against my belly. It warmed me, fed me. Our bodies felt like one, his thighs glued to mine.

"I think we need to try all the flavors," he said, gasping for breath. He kissed my neck and face, his whole body hugging mine.

Yeah, we did. Ciertamente.

Our ardor slaked . . . for now . . . we threw on swim shorts and went to check on the kids. Marcus and Violetta had made very good castles, which Primo kept kicking down, jumping up and down with pleasure. Mio picked him up and swung him around.

"Did I win?" Marcus kept asking as we took the kids for their second swim that day. They were both excellent swimmers. They should have been. I'd taught them myself. Belen showed up from a meeting with her attorney. I was beginning to wonder about her and that man. She seemed to be spending a lot of time with him.

Back at the apartment, we bathed the kids, re-dressing them with some of the clothes we kept in our second bed-room, now theirs, for their frequent stay overs. Belen sat down to watch TV with them. Marcus raced off to his apartment to shower and change. It was while Mio and I bathed that he revealed his plan.

"It's going to be our anniversary soon," he said. "In a few weeks, it will be one year since we met . . . since I knew I had to be with you."

I grinned. "You didn't always feel that way."

"Yes, I did." He kissed me under the spray of warm wa-ter, his hands moving over my body. "So, I've been think-ing . . . We should go to Cuba."

"What?" I said, stunned.

"Cuba. You once told me it was the place you always wanted to go and . . . I've been thinking, I miss being a whore, and —"

"You . . . what?"

"Will you relax? I'm your whore. Don't get me wrong . . . I am glad I'm your little . . . pit pony, but you must admit I am very good at being very bad. I like being your wild stal-lion."

"Where are you going with this?"

"I want to be your whore. Let me plan a little . . . forbidden liaison . . . a little sexy fun for us. I know a place we can stay . . . I'll arrange everything as if you are my best, most expensive client and I have to work very hard to please you. We don't have much time, but we could squeeze in say . . . five days? To celebrate our anniversary properly, you know."

He glanced down, and his voice turned to a purr. "Why, Evans . . . I see you like that idea a lot." His soapy hands gripped my now rigid cock, and he stroked me.

God help me, I did like the idea. I grinned like a big galoot as his hands gripped our cocks, sliding them back and forth against his palms. They rubbed against one another. He held me, and I held his face, kissing him.

I loved the sensation of our cocks colliding, his hand coaxing me to pleasure. He knew all the places to touch me as he stroked, his tongue raking across my collarbone, a hot spot for me. My breathing became shallow, my desire for his orgasm almost stronger than my own. I touched him, and he gasped as my fingers curled around his shaft. Feeling our cocks trapped between both of our hands was too much. With my free hand, I gripped the wall of the shower stall as he suddenly bent and licked me. I came hard, Mio rising so I could hold him.

Our heads clunked.

"Ow." He started laughing as he came, my fingers still wrapped around his shaft. He fucked my fist. I wanted him inside me. I always wanted him inside me. Now I had him all over me. He kissed me as water streamed down our bodies. His hands fell from my cock and slid behind me to hold my ass. I could feel his hard cock still twitching against my belly. It was an amazing way to kick off our evening's festivities.

* * *

The kids were hungry, and after a family vote, we decided on the Pink Elephant for dinner. It didn't open until seven o'clock, which I used to think was late for small children, but things in Barcelona were different. Restaurants closed at four after a three-hour lunch service and opened again at eight or nine for dinner, closing again in the wee hours of the morning.

Our pair was used to this. The kids were wide awake and, as usual in public, very well behaved. They walked down the street holding our hands. Marcus and Primo loved the restaurant's chicken fingers, which they served with honey dipping sauce.

"Maybe the strawberry and goat cheese risotto for me," Belen said, glued to her cell phone as always.

"I want crab cakes," my little Violetta said. I picked her up and held her. Mio swung Primo into his arms. I wanted them to eat whatever they wanted. No mac and cheese for our kids tonight. At the restaurant, we pushed through the crowd gathered around the bar. Mio found us a table in the back, two pushed together, the black leather chairs as comfy as ever. We settled the kids in their seats and Primo stared around the room at the pink walls we all loved. Gilt-framed mirrors and vintage paintings gave a homey feel to the place.

We knew the waiter who rushed to our table. He insisted on bringing us appetizers of coconut shrimp.

"I have something special for the bebés," he said, running off and returning with three tiny scoops of cotton candy ice cream. The kids' favorite. All three of them.

"Oh, boy!" Marcus and Violetta said in unison. Primo dropped his face to his plate and began to lick. I stared at my lover, who tried desperately not to laugh. Primo had picked up that little trick from Mio.

Belen slapped her brother's arm. "I remember that trick. You taught it to me."

"Aren't I a lovely brother?" he teased.

"No. You're ridiculous. Primo!"

The little boy lifted his face. Mio wiped it with a napkin and kissed the kid's nose.

"Tasty," he said.

Primo nodded, his eyes widening in appreciation when he saw the shrimp arriving. I couldn't wait for our little sexy vacation, but a part of me was already fretting about leaving the kids. I loved them. I told myself it was only five days . . . but I dreaded coming home and learning they'd eaten nothing but macaroni in our absence. I'd have to talk to Mio's mother and get her to watch over their meals.

"You having fun?" Mio asked, watchful and clearly worried.

I smiled, wanting to encourage him. "Of course," I said. "I'm already thinking about dessert. And I don't mean ice cream."

The look on his face made me happy, oh so happy that he was my man. I wondered what secrets he was planning for us as we hoed into our fabulous meal. I had to pinch myself at how lucky I was. I would be going home with the man of my dreams.

Marcus, who would never hurt a butterfly, would, when all was said and done, be going home alone. He kept his cell phone at his elbow, but it was becoming obvious that Jaime was otherwise occupied.

I made sure Marcus got extra bread rolls, a nice, big cocktail and a generous slice of chocolate cake for dessert.

"You're like a mama bear with him," Mio said when we tucked the kids into bed later.

"Does it bother you?" I asked, anxiously.

"Guapo, I think it is very cute. And before you ask, he will survive five days without us."

I loved Mio's family and always enjoyed seeing his mother, who did like me, but I am sure would have preferred a pretty, childbearing Spanish girl for her son instead of an American man. She had recently begun to tell me, though, that she always knew her son preferred men.

"Thank Saint Maria he picked you!" she'd said more than once.

Mio's problem—and mine—was his father. His old man liked me. Really liked me. But he was an odd mix of grouchy old man and impish child. He and his twin brother had recently given up running their local grocery store and now drove their wives nuts by being home all day.

We were encouraged to spend time with them, that is, get them out of the house, but Mio and his dad would argue, and I tended to lose the old geezer. No matter what he and I did together, he always managed to vanish. The first time I was frantic and almost called the police. The second time I caught him sneaking away and gave up trying to wrestle him away from his living room sofa.

He genuinely seemed to enjoy Marcus however. They liked to play cards, and I suspect Marcus lost most of the time, but as soon as we arrived for Sunday lunch, they slipped out to the back garden for a game of poker.

I stood in the kitchen, drooling over all the delicious smells wafting from the pots, pans and covered baking dishes along the sideboard. Mama explained each dish to me. They all sounded good. I was sorry however that there wasn't any turkey since I'd mastered that phrase since yesterday. I helped her set the table as Belen picked at the keys on her cell phone, frowning.

"Do you think my attorney could possibly be married?" she asked. "He's so unavailable on weekends."

"I think he is exhausted. You're a handful. Like me," Mio said, lazily biting into an artichoke heart stuffed with ham.

"Give the man a rest."

Belen cocked a brow in his direction, then swiveled her gaze at me. "Is Mio a handful?"

"Of course not."

"There goes that theory," Belen told her brother and kept tapping at her keys.

Mio shot me a reproachful look. "Why did you say that? I like thinking I have your mind fully occupied."

"You do," I assured him. He gave me a happy smile and picked up an asparagus spear.

The children came running the moment the hot food hit the table. I was so busy arranging things prettily that I made it to table a minute after everybody else. I slid to first base . . . er . . . my seat, beside Mio as dishes started flying around. The artichokes were gone before I could grab one. My fork just missed the asparagus. Mama's stuffed avocadoes whizzed by me, and I screamed.

"I. Want. Food!"

Everyone stopped and stared at me.

"Guapo," my lover said, his eyes wide. "Your Spanish . . . it's getting so good!"

I had no idea I'd spoken in Spanish, but I must have impressed his father who passed me one of the artichokes he was hoarding on his plate. Primo gave me two asparagus spears. Marcus very kindly gave me a slice of tomato and Mio spooned some other yummy looking things onto my plate and gave me a smile that guaranteed good things in the bedroom later.

Marcus wasn't so lucky, however. That evening, he learned about his relationship break-up on Twitter. Jaime had posted numerous photos to his account via Instagram, the hot new photo-sharing tool a lot of tweeters had started to use because, unlike Twitpic, Twitter's official photo uploader, the results aren't scrutinized for pornographic content leading to canceled accounts.

And the photos of Jaime and Dino were not only explicit, they were devastating. Marcus couldn't sleep. He sobbed over his laptop, now parked at our dining room table, as Jaime kept uploading photos and increasingly acerbic comments about what a loser Marcus was. At two a.m. Mio gave him a Valium, which he took, but it hardly made a dent in his wakeful state. On the contrary, he just seemed to sob more. Mio and I read the nonstop parade of tweets. I was mortified, and they weren't even about me.

The captions all read, "My new love," and "My new man." Marcus went berserk over one tweet that read, "Finally, I know what it is to be with a real man."

"What's that supposed to mean?" Marcus shrieked.

Mio and I had no idea. To his credit, he listened to us and didn't retaliate with a single tweet, snarky text or hysterical cell phone message.

We tried to get him to stop reading, but he couldn't help himself. We didn't want to get in the middle of things, but we had to when Marcus' cell phone began to ring, and we learned that Jaime had called the two production companies the couple had worked for shooting gay porn. Both now wanted to cancel Marcus' contracts. We listened in growing horror as the reps told Marcus that Jaime had told them Marcus was unstable and a drug user and worse . . . he was secretly straight. The gay porn companies dropped him like a hot brick.

"Mio, do something," I implored. And then his cell phone rang. It was Jaime, asking him to pack his bags and send them to Paris. He was moving in with Dino.

I have never heard the kind of language Mio hurled at the man coming out of his mouth before. Marcus sat, mouth open, tears rolling down his cheeks as Mio told Jaime he wouldn't do a thing to help him unless he deleted all the inflammatory tweets and called off the porn pit bulls.

"We'll have a yard sale and sell off all your Nasty Pig clothing." Mio must have known how Jaime would react.

"He hung up on me," Mio said. The next thing that happened was that my cell phone rang.

"Don't answer it," Mio commanded. "We are not playing good cop, bad cop."

"Of course not," I agreed.

Marcus gave us a wan smile. "You're such good friends."

When I didn't pick up, Jaime called Mio again.

I could hear him screaming, "Don't you touch my clothes!"

"I am going to wear your Industry hoodies. Oh, yes. I am going to wear them, and then I'm going to give them to the first homeless woman I see on the streets. Delete the tweets, guapo, or else."

Guapo. He'd never called Jaime that. I blinked. I knew my man well, and it finally occurred to me that he and Jaime must have, at some point, been lovers. The thought infiltrated my brain with a mindless rage I fought to tamp down. This wasn't about me now. Whatever happened between Jaime and Mio, it must have been before me. A long time ago. I focused on taking deep breaths as Mio negotiated the Great Tweet Takedown. The only tweets left by the time Mio had promised to cut up Jaime's favorite jockstraps were the ones announcing his new love . . . and his decision to no longer shoot gay porn with anyone other than Dino Martino.

"Oh my God, is he joking?" Marcus wiped snot from his upper lip with the back of his hand. "He's committing career suicide."

"Let him." Mio looked grumpy as he reached for my hand. "Come on, guapo, we need some sleep. Tomorrow, we have to pack Jaime's things and send them to him." He looked at Marcus. "He's letting you keep the furniture. He just wants his clothes."

Marcus snorted. "That's big of him. We don't own the furniture. We rented the place fully furnished."

Mio shrugged. He was now in a very strange mood, which eclipsed my fury about his possible past association with Jaime.

Marcus began to yawn. It was four o'clock in the morning, and we were all exhausted. He gave us a wave and parked his ass on our sofa, covering his curled-up body with Primo's Spiderman throw.

In our bedroom, Mio paced the floor. "He's such an asshole." Hands on hips his pacing grew more aggressive. "I have to go out for a run." I opened my mouth. He held up a hand. "Alone."

I let him go. We did everything together. Especially running. We did this primarily to police each other . . . alone we'd be sneaking into bakeries scarfing pastries. This was weird. I knew he was terribly upset and wondered if Jaime was somebody he'd loved once. If so, how much? I sat on the edge of our bed, wondering what was going through his mind . . . would he tell me? Mio was a passionate man. The most ardent lover I'd ever had. He was committed to me, I knew that. But there were things about his past he'd never revealed. I have no idea how long I'd been sitting there but our bedroom door opened and he was back. Dripping wet, shaking with exertion . . . and something else. Emotion.

"Mio?" I got up and went straight to him. He grabbed me and held me. We stood like that, heat transferring back and forth between us. It confused me at first because apart from the moment when he'd come to claim me in Los Angeles I'd never seen him . . . broken. It stunned me. Something made me hold him tighter. I kissed his shoulder and sensed the tension ebbing from his body.

"I hate how I feel." He sounded so small and so forlorn. I didn't know where to begin getting him to talk. I'd never seen him like this. I said nothing and just kept holding him.

"You know, don't you?" he asked. He turned his head, his lips finding a spot on my neck. He was burning up.

I began to rub his back. I wanted to know, but didn't really. Did I want the gory details of how much he'd loved another man before me?

He pulled away. He left our room and came back with two snifters of cognac. He shut the door with his butt and sat away from me, on the chaise where we'd had some pretty great sex — numerous times.

Mio didn't look at me as he held my glass out to me. I took it. I didn't know what to do with myself, so I stood, leaning against the wall. It felt . . . wrong somehow to sit on the bed I shared with him, hearing him talking about his relationship with somebody else.

I waited.

"He was the first man I ever loved."

I was stunned. Neither of them had ever given an indication of it.

"The first man." He repeated the words, then took a sip of his drink. "He was the first man I was ever with. I was nineteen and thought . . . I thought he was a god, that we'd be together forever, then he dumped me. In those days, there was no Twitter. No . . . Instagram. He sent two men to the apartment we shared. They took everything. Even things that belonged to me. They beat me, kicked me, knocked me unconscious. My uncle saved my life. He found me. He took me home. It took me a long time physically to get over what he did to me. Emotionally it took longer. I decided I would never love again. And I didn't."

He said nothing for a few minutes. Anger seeped into his lovely eyes. "I went to college and studied, but I was obsessed with what he'd done to me. I felt ugly . . . unlovable. And then I began to sleep around. I went into porn. I didn't like it, and it embarrassed my family. Some families have secrets, but mine . . . you are aware of what they're like. Being an escort was more private and, as you know, I was able to make a lot more money."

Mio sipped his drink again and winced. "It burns." He glanced up at me. "Like Jaime. He pursued me the whole time. For years. I knew he had lovers. He was always in love, but he was also chasing after me. When I wanted to give up making movies, we did my final one together. Alejandro's farewell."

Alejandro had been Mio's porn name. I'd never seen his movies . . . I'd seen a couple of photos, a few clips, but couldn't handle seeing the movies themselves, so I'd never realized he'd been in one with Jaime.

"What was it like making the movie with him after everything that happened?"

He leaned forward, his gaze holding mine.

"It felt like nothing. I was nervous. I couldn't sleep the night before. I had three scenes to shoot with him and a threesome. I thought I had to be crazy fucking the man who'd crushed my heart. He'd chased me for ten years, and we got big money for that movie and . . . bam! Nothing."

He looked surprised as he swished the contents of his glass around. "I didn't have feelings for him. I didn't want him. I didn't hate him. I fucked him." He grinned. "That felt good. That felt right."

Mio's face crumpled for a moment. "I was finally free. I took care of my clients. I did my job. I thought I'd make enough money and retire with young boyfriends in every town or something . . . but you changed all that."

"You wanted young boyfriends in every town?"

He shrugged. "I wanted sex. I wanted companionship. I

did not want to love again and damn you . . . you did it. You made me change my mind. I gave up everything and I — I've never been happier, Evans. I wasn't really free of Jaime until the day you said you'd be my man."

I couldn't respond to that. I'd never known any of it. I'd had no clue. I had no idea how he'd dealt with Jaime being in our lives, but I understood now why he funneled Jaime and Marcus some sex business and kept them at arm's length . . . well, Jaime anyway. Marcus had crawled into our hearts from the broken edge of the screen door. He'd allowed me to have Marcus as a friend because —

"You knew Jaime would hurt him, didn't you?"

Mio drained his drink. "Oh, yes. Which is why we are going to pack all of that . . . that culo's things and ship them to him. And" — a dramatic pause — "we are going to move Marcus into a different apartment. He couldn't take Jaime coming after him and hurting him."

"You think he'd do that?"

"I know he will."

"Where will we put him?"

Mio smiled at me. "With my parents. Jaime would never touch him with my parents looking after him. Don't forget, he has unfinished business with my father, who still wants to kill him. Besides, nobody but us will know where he is."

"You think he's safe there?"

"Of course. And Jaime won't be able to contact us because we will be in Cuba. I will be too busy being your hot whore-boy to talk to him."

I smiled then. "And I'll be too busy, too, I take it?"

"Evans McCoy, soon to be Cortez, if you have time to do anything with your hands on this vacation, then I would not be doing my job."

"And you still want to go?"

He stared at me incredulously. "Let me show you how

much." He dropped his drink on the nightstand, relieved me of mine and pushed me to the bed. He needed me so much that it took my breath away. I'd never loved him more than in that moment.

"Evans, Evans," he kept saying over and over. "I have to lick you. I have to kiss you."

He removed all my clothing. I was hard as a rock. His eyes gleamed with tears as I pushed away his clothes, my hands finally making contact with his beautiful, smooth-caramel skin. He didn't cry; he blinked away the tears.

"Thank God I found you," he said, looking down at me as he knelt between my wide-open thighs and plunged his gorgeous cock into me. He made love to me slowly, gently, but with the same, driving force he always did. He wanted to possess me, own me completely. I wanted the same thing. His knowledge of my body, my heart, his own desires fused and fueled me. I'd never wanted him more. We came together, a crashing, crushing orgasm that left me feeling as if I'd just been on one wild ride. He collapsed on top of me, his heartbeat erratic as I wrapped my arms and legs around him. We dozed and I prayed that he would never come out of me.

The last thing he said as he fell asleep with his damp head clamped to my shoulder was, "Tesoro."

CHAPTER THREE

Marcus packed his stuff and moved in with Mama Cortez without a whimper the next morning. Mio was busy making furtive phone calls as he helped me stuff Jaime's things into suitcases. I was shocked at how untidy Jaime was. And how dirty. Obviously, filthy clothing had been thrown into shopping bags and suitcases with items that still had labels on them.

I think Marcus liked us fussing over him. Belen took the kids to Mama and came over to help clean and make coffee. I'd never seen the cell phone out of her hands for so long. For a moment she and Mio whispered to one another in the kitchen. They were up to something.

Mio walked her to her car. I suspected he was worried Jaime's goons might show up. When he returned, he confiscated Marcus' cell phone and laptop, and after one last sweep of the apartment, Marcus left it for the last time. He followed us in his little Fiat to Mama's, where I stood with amusement watching the big galoot extricate himself from the tiny vehicle. Mio took the keys and parked the car inside the garage, then padlocked the door.

Inside the house, Mio instructed his mother to feed Marcus nonstop. She was in heaven, and so was he. Mio and I said we'd be back for lunch, drove home and handed Marcus' keys to the landlady who managed a lot of the apartments in the complex.

She told us she'd read about the ugly bust-up online and it surprised me. Even decrepit old ladies had now gone digital.

"Where is he moving to?" she asked. She tried to keep her tone casual but seemed way too excited for it to be anything but a pointed question.

"He's visiting friends out of town," Mio said.

"What friends? Where?"

Mio shrugged. Lord, I wished I could soon master that most expressive form of Spanish. It said nothing, invited even less and effectively stopped all questions.

We shipped Jaime's suitcases to Paris via a very cool website called luggageforward.com, locked our doors and windows, set the alarm and went off to Mama's for lunch.

"What's happening on the Internet?" Marcus asked us around a mouthful of mantecado, Spanish crumble cookies. They were Mama's specialty. I felt very resentful. She was my Mama-in-law, and she made mantecado for me. Not that I said so, of course. I worried that I'd been replaced and then felt terrible. Poor Marcus . . . he needed Mama's healing heart. Belen and the kids arrived for lunch, throwing themselves into my arms. I was ecstatic to see them. Next thing I knew, there was great excitement. Mio had arranged to fly us all to Fort Lauderdale, Florida for a week.

"Florida?" Belen was ecstatic. "I've always wanted to go there."

"Good because we're leaving tonight." Mio was having a whale of a time being secretive with his cell phone conversations. He disappeared into the garden with Papa Cortez. Later, as Marcus and I wrestled over the last cookie, Papa walked into the kitchen, commanding Mama to pack.

"Come on, guapo," Mio said to me. "We have to get ready."

"Eat first," his mother said. I ran to the table and grabbed my fork.

"Evans, you are becoming so Spanish." Mio grinned and

kissed me.

Marcus was so happy to be included in the trip that he forgot to be miserable until he sneaked a peek at Belen's cell phone. He saw that his former paramour was still saying disparaging things about him online.

"He's such an ass," Mio said. "Don't respond. Don't get involved. And don't, whatever you do tell him or anybody where we're going."

"Okay, Mio. I'll be a good boy."

Mio snatched the phone away from him and handed it to Belen. "He's like a junkie. This is crack. He can't have it. Okay?"

Belen nodded. She returned to her furious texting. "I'm checking out the nightclubs in Fort Lauderdale. Marcus said he'd take me."

Mio and I exchanged looks. Those two together would get into trouble for sure.

Primo clung to my legs and wept as I tried to leave.

"Come and play cards," Papa said to him. He took Marcus in one hand, Primo in the other.

We made our escape as Belen hugged me quickly, saying, "How nice Primo has somebody his own age to play with!"

On the drive home, Mio held my hand.

"Do you worry about Jaime sending people here to beat us up?" I asked over the noise of the wind and music. As usual, Mio drove with the top down, and Britney cranked high.

"Yes," he said. "I've experienced his break-up technique, but guapo what concerns me is not who he might send here and what they might do . . . but what I will do to them. If anyone ever tried to hurt you, I would kill them."

At the apartment, we jumped into bed for a hot, quick romp, then ran around getting ready. I kept thinking about our conversation in the car.

He had a gun somewhere in the apartment, well hidden because of the children. The idea of men coming after us was chilling. I was glad we were leaving town that night.

Mio must have realized I was worried. Perhaps it was the way I kept glancing out the windows.

"You seriously think I'd let anybody near our front door?" He looked so offended I had to put on my best game face.

"No," I said, because the truth was, I trusted him. I felt safe with him. He kissed me, then glanced at his watch. "Let's go. Our flight leaves in a couple of hours."

He grinned at me; my hot little whore was back in da house. "We spend one day in Florida and then you and me . . . Cuba, baby."

I couldn't help smiling, too. "Is Cuba gay-friendly?"

"So-so. It is accepted, and in some parts, there are gay accommodations. One man I know runs a casa particular exclusively for gay couples."

"Have you stayed there?"

He looked pained. "Once. I traveled with a client. And although I like the host I have no intentions of taking you to someone's home. We're going in style. I am trying to decide between two resorts. My favorite one is not very . . . as you call it, gay-friendly. The other one is."

"Well, we are having a forbidden liaison aren't we?"

He laughed. "Si, but there is forbidden, and there is needlessly difficult. There is no reason for that. It's hard enough for me that you are a straight, married man running away for a little fun with me. We have to be careful your wife doesn't find out."

"Wait . . . that's your fantasy? That I'm a straight married man?"

"I used to adore fucking allegedly straight men."

The look on his face was mournful.

"You miss it." I wasn't sure if I should feel wounded or not.

He shrugged. "No. I miss the sneakiness. The planning." His eyes gleamed. "I like that I am sneaking around dreaming up the perfect, sexy vacation for you." He kissed me. "Cuba, here we come."

We flew out that night from Barcelona to Atlanta on Air France. Mio had booked the whole family into first class. I didn't want to think about how much it cost. It was a gentle reminder of traveling to Barcelona to visit Mio the first time. This time we were together with the thing I'd always wanted . . . a family.

Primo and Violetta invaded our seats and forced us to watch the Transformers movie. Twice. Primo pretended to be scared and huddled into me, but he'd seen it several times already. He figured out the buttons and dials, asked for chocolate milk three times, but always managed to remember to say "please," then fell asleep in Mio's arms. Violetta spent an hour telling me about a dream she'd had. I could tell she visited wonderful worlds in her sleeping state. I wanted to help her remember them, to use them. I sensed she would be a remarkable writer one day.

Mio reached for my hand, the kids snuggled between us. Belen came to check on us, tucking the Spiderman throw around us.

"I really wish Marcus was straight," she whispered to me. Mio pretended to be asleep. I didn't know what to say and wished I'd beaten him to the ruse.

In Atlanta, we switched planes for the final leg of our journey to the Fort Lauderdale-Hollywood airport. Mio had booked three king penthouse suites at the Atlantic Hotel and Spa. We shared one with Marcus, Belen, and the kids had one, and Mio's parents took up the third. His mother was ecstatic when she saw the ocean front view, the verandah with chairs, a table, sunken bathtubs and mirrors . . . a personal valet for her and Papa—and then she realized there was no kitchen.

"You're not cooking," Mio told her. "And now you and Belen must have your facials."

He'd arranged a massage for his father and for Marcus, who was in paroxysms of anxiety over threatening texts he'd received from Jaime. Mio told him to ignore them.

We read them over his shoulder. Jaime was going crazy that Marcus had moved out without telling him where he was going. He'd received his suitcases, so why was he terrorizing his former lover?

"He's so angry, and I don't know why."

"Stop reading the damned texts." Mio yanked the phone from his hands, left Marcus in the masseur's custody and that left us free to take the kids down to the pool. Primo was so excited. I was going to miss my sweet little nephew the next few days, but I knew he'd have plenty to distract him. The resort was fabulous.

Nobody was pleased we were leaving the following morning, but Mio had arranged for loads of activities for them and I . . . well, as I got ready for dinner that evening, I received a note from our valet, George. He was a lovely man who'd been run ragged by Mama, Papa, and the kids but seemed to love it. George held a silver tray in his hands containing an envelope. Beside it sat the most delicious looking pastry I'd ever seen.

"For you, Señor McCoy. This is a pastelito de guayaba, a guava pastry fresh from Cuba. It is sent with love from your husband."

Mio was taking a shower, so I couldn't throw myself at him. I took the pastry and my note. As much as I wanted to inhale the gauzy confection on the spot, I knew it would be tastier in bed with Mio later. I tried to tip the valet, but he backed away.

"Señor Cortez would kill me." He gave me a slight bow and left. I put the pastry in the fridge so the kids wouldn't scarf it and stepped outside to read my note. The sky was a soft, velvety lilac. Palm trees swayed across the boardwalk below. We'd been here all day, and I hadn't set foot on the beach. My fingertips traced Mio's writing on the thick, cream-colored envelope. One word. Tesoro.

I turned it over. I hated to break the wax seal on it, but I had to know its contents. In the early days of our courtship, Mio and I, long-distance lovers, had exchanged feverish faxes. I still have each and every one of them. He still sends me love letters . . . but it's been a while. I sat on one of the chairs on the balcony and slid out three sheets of Mio's parchment paper.

Evans,

I was rereading Don Quixote last night as you slept beside me on the plane. I watched you for a while, but I longed to talk to you, and so I decided to read to keep me from disturbing you. I love our new habit of reading together. I love listening to your voice as you tell me a story. I enjoy helping you explore Don Quixote in Spanish, a far superior version than the English. I wanted to find a special passage for our next book session. I have downloaded the book onto my iPhone, and I devour little bits here and there since our favorite madman is such a big part of our lives.

My life was insanity without you. It would be worse if it were to ever become so empty again. I know now that I just could not cope, so it's interesting that my eyes fell on this passage:

"For what I want of Dulcinea del Toboso she is as good as the greatest princess in the land. For not all those poets who praise ladies under names which they choose so freely, really have such mistresses . . ."

I realized I had told you that before we met my plan was to have

45

many men . . . many lovers, so I would love nobody. I can't even imagine that life now. I can't imagine not waking up to your beautiful face beside me. I cannot stand to think of a life where I don't look for the perfect roses for you, the perfect pastry, not doing something to make you smile. I told you I loved Jaime once and feel proud that you never guessed our previous relationship. I always made it clear to him that I didn't want you to know. I prize your happiness. I guard it fiercely. I never thought I would ever meet one man who could be everything to me.

You are above and beyond anyone I have ever met, talked to . . . seen on a movie screen. You are so wonderful that I pinch myself a thousand times a day. I wanted to let Jaime go, with love, affection. I wanted him to be free. I wanted him to find what I have found with you. I thought for a time he could be happy with Marcus, that he could stop seeking outside of himself to fill all the holes he has inside.

I now no longer care. I have tried. And I must turn my back on him. He can never be near us again. He can't be a part of our lives, and I hope you can understand that.

You have given me a peace and joy I never knew before. I keep thinking it cannot be possible to be so happy even as I wake every morning, look at the sky and say thank you. I whisper my gratitude into the wind. I love you forever and never want to let you go. My hands always want to be on you. You are my Dulcinea, my prince. My whole heart. My tesoro.

Mio.

I sat on the balcony and wept. One teardrop fell on the last page and made a black splotch. I tried to blot it and heard him come outside to me.

"Guapismo?" He hunkered beside me. "What's wrong? Why—" He saw that I was holding his note and gave me the sweetest smile. "That wasn't supposed to make you cry. I agonized over this, wondering if I should even mention Jaime in a love letter to you—"

I threw myself at him. He fell back as I covered his face with kisses. I worried that he'd hit his head, then wanted him so badly I couldn't think of anything else. His hands were at my belt. Mine were at his. We kissed and licked each other's mouths, hungry for closer contact. Somebody whistled, and I broke off our kiss. I'd just realized we had a glass balcony and everyone could see us below.

"Don't stop now," he urged. His lusty smile showed me that he wanted me badly, too. I wrestled his pants down, and his delicious cock sprang free.

"Dude," said a voice. I was about to start sucking Mio when I turned. Marcus was standing on our balcony.

"What the fuck!" I screamed.

"Primo said you were attacking Mio." He gave us a shaka sign. "But I see he's a . . . er . . . willing victim." He didn't move. He just stood there. Watching.

"Get out of here!" Mio started to laugh in the next breath when George rushed out and dragged Marcus away.

"Maybe we should go inside," I said, trying hard to swallow my disappointment.

Mio pushed at me with gentle hands. "Attack me in our bedroom."

I got up, held my hand to him and helped him up. I soon forgot our disrupted rhythm as he pushed me against the wall and kissed me. Hard.

His cock raged between us, Mio fumbling for my pants. The moment his hand curled around my shaft, I thought I would come on the spot. He gave me a wicked grin, grabbed my shirt collar and hauled me inside.

On the bed, we fought the constraints of shoes and clothing. We were left with our socks on, too famished for one another to keep up the striptease. I straddled his body. I let my ass ride his thighs, allowing his cock to move back and forth along my crack.

"In," he moaned. "Let me in." I ignored him. I knew that having me ride him was one of his favorite ways to fuck me. He was anxious. He was hot. And I wouldn't let up. I raised my hips. He grabbed his cock and rubbed the head against my hole as I gazed down into his eyes. Desire, need, love . . . I saw it all.

"Let me in," he begged.

"Mio, get me ready for you." He lost no time in flipping me onto my back and licking my ass. Nobody had ever eaten me the way he did. He spent hours pleasuring me. For the first time in our relationship, however, I wanted him to be quick.

"Hurry, Mio."

"So impatient, Evans." He lifted his face, put a kiss on my thigh, then went right back to work. He knew me well enough to leave my cock and balls alone. One tiny flick of his tongue across those danger zones and I'd come before he could even get inside me. Too late. I'd started leaking. I almost said something, but he already knew. He raised his face away from me and with a predatory gleam in his eyes eagerly pounced on my cock.

He sucked me until he'd caught every last drop. "I want to wait," he said as he took his mouth from me, "but I can't." He rolled onto his back, and I mounted him again. He furrowed his brow in concentration as he sought to gain entry into me. Without lube it was harder but oh, so rewarding. I took over as his cock head nestled against me. I moved my hips the way I knew he liked. He started to go crazy.

"Oh, tesoro . . ."

I worked him into me, Mio's fingers on my thighs, my ass, reaching down to stroke my feet. He raised his head to kiss me and rained kisses down my throat and chest. He wisely avoided my nipples and only briefly cuffed my cock in his fist as I kept moving up and down on him.

Our eyes locked when his cock started to slide into me. Deeper and deeper, he invaded me, and I lost all words. Nothing mattered. I was aware of knocking but could only respond to his touch, his hot mouth on mine. He gripped my ass with one hand, my cock with the other and began to stroke me with a tight hold.

God, it felt like Heaven and Hell. I loved the way he fucked me. I was about to come but couldn't fight it. I wanted to reach euphoria but didn't want him to stop plunging into me. He knew how to drive me, however, and said in a gruff tone, "Venido a por mi. Ahora! Come for me. Now!" We came together, my body quaking atop his muscular thighs. I held on, Mio's hands gripping me to him. I ground down one last time, and he held my hips steady. He gazed up at me, smiling.

"Being with you means I never have to go to Euro Disney," he said, making me laugh. I didn't want to leave our bed, but we were having a family dinner.

"I am going to spoil you this week," he promised. "That's the only reason I'm willing to share you tonight."

As we showered together and dressed again, I wondered what plans he had in store for us in Cuba. He had been so mysterious, but I was excited. As I slipped on my socks and shoes, the children came running. Primo had chocolate smeared all over his face. He dragged me to the living room of Mama and Papa's suite where George had set a beautiful table for eight. Mama and Papa were already eating. George explained to us that he was here to make anything and everything each of us wanted. I loved it. This was a wonderful way for everyone to relax but still be together enjoying a leisurely meal.

"What can I get for you?" he asked me. Primo tugged at George's pants.

George gazed down at him. "What can I get for you, Señor Primo?" He spoke fluent Spanish. Primo and Violetta giggled.

"Pancakes," they said in unison. It must have seemed like the most exotic thing in the world to them, American pancakes.

The kids looked at me. They wanted me to have pancakes, too.

"Pancakes sound great," I said as Primo squirreled up my right leg and into my arms. Violetta pouted until Mio picked her up.

"I'd like a steak," he said. "Thank you, George, but please, feed the children first."

We joined Mama and Papa at the table.

Mama smiled at me. She was in orbit. So far she'd eaten chicken, fish, an omelet, some soft shell crab and now she was pondering dessert. I laughed. It was a wonderful treat for her. She was so used to being the one who conjured magic in the kitchen, now she was enjoying a well-earned rest. Knowing George was here to cater to her every whim made me relax. Mio and I could slip away for a few days without worrying about the family.

"What do you think?" she asked me. "Chocolate soufflé or cheesecake?"

"You're asking me to choose? You can't choose. You must try both."

"My thoughts exactly." When I caught the last word, exactamente, it was only then that I realized I'd conversed quite fluently with her in Spanish. I felt proud when I caught my lover's radiant smile.

George brought three plates of pancakes to the table. Primo wouldn't move from my lap so I ate around him. He doctored mine heavily with warm chocolate syrup and whipped cream. The kid was a gourmand.

Violetta preferred bananas and berries with warm coconut syrup. She offered me a bite. Hers was so tasty I asked for more pancakes so I could dine Violetta-style. Mio and Primo shared a medium steak and debated over dessert when Marcus and Belen crashed into the room.

"We saw Jaime on TV," Marcus said, his eyes alight. Mio shook his head. Marcus stopped speaking. Mio never liked emotional discussions in front of the children or his parents.

"Sit, eat," he said. Marcus and Belen obeyed and soon relaxed as George prepared them each a blackberry mimosa.

Only after dinner was over and Mama was bathing the kids did Marcus get to spill his news.

"They pulled him off a flight in Paris. He was flying to Barcelona. He was apparently really drunk, and he fought with a flight attendant."

"Where is he now?" I asked.

Belen said, "He's been calling Marcus. They held him at the airport for a while. They charged him but released him on bail. Last text Marcus got, he said they let him go, but he's due in court in two days." She glanced at Mio. "He asked Marcus to go to London."

I didn't know what to say. Mio didn't seem surprised though.

"Marcus," he suddenly said, "Do you have money?"

Marcus shrugged. "Yeah."

"A lot?"

"Yeah."

Mio nodded. "So, you've been taking care of him."

Marcus's cheeks flamed. "Well . . . he does some movies and some escorting . . ."

"Hey, you're talking to me now. There's not a lot of money in porn movies. I know. It was changing when I quit. There's definitely money in escort work, I know that myself. But I also know how you live. You're not exactly frugal."

"All right." Marcus seemed deflated now. "I take care of

him. What's that got to do with anything?"

"Why's he asking you to fly to London if he's still with Dino Martino?"

"Because . . . well . . . because . . . they probably broke up! He loves me!"

"So why's he still tweeting about Dino?"

"He what?" Marcus looked incredulous.

"Missing my bf." Mio showed him his cell phone.

"Maybe that's . . . me?"

"No." Mio shook his head. "Dino's tweeting him back. They were on the flight together. Dino is doing a club show Saturday night in Barcelona."

"He does?" Marcus looked stunned.

Mio must have been following all of this. "Yeah. He's the star performer in a leather show at Berlin Dark."

Marcus swallowed hard. I could see his Adam's apple bobbing. His face seemed to pale. "I know. He was supposed to do that show with me."

"Not anymore." Mio pressed numbers on his phone and showed it to Marcus. He looked devastated.

"I booked that show. I did the poster art!" Marcus shrieked.

I took the phone from Mio's hands and examined it. Sure enough, Marcus had been Photoshopped out of the picture, and Dino Martino was in. I studied the captions. I was so out of the singles loop I'd had no idea that Saturday night would kick off a gigantic, week-long GLBT circuit party in Barcelona.

"So . . ." Marcus was trying to pull himself together. Belen had her arms around him, kissing his head. "He wanted me to come to London and do what . . . pay his legal expenses?"

"Did he ask you to?" Mio was nothing if not direct.

"He said he'd pay me back."

"How much money does he already owe you?"

"A lot."

Mio shook his head. "Dino has money. I know that for a fact. He has a lucrative day job in graphic design. That's where the money is these days."

"I know." Marcus looked depressed.

"That's how you made your money?" Belen looked surprised.

"I got an inheritance. I put it into my business." Marcus frowned. "I like sex, so I started doing porn. I've always been able to do both." He glanced at Mio. "If you hadn't told me this . . . I wouldn't have looked at Twitter. He's been lying to me. Playing me for a fool."

Nobody said anything for a moment. "He probably always has," he muttered, stating what was probably on everyone's minds. "And to think I almost stopped all my design work to be available to that . . . that . . . culo."

He ran from the room. "I'll go talk to him," Belen said, hurrying after him.

"Is she developing a crush on him?" I asked Mio.

"Yes and no. She's always liked men who are reclamation projects." He took my hand. "We have to read to the children. We'll say goodnight. In the morning, I have to leave early."

"What!"

"I am your whore, remember? I fly ahead to Cuba and arrange everything. I'll be there waiting for you."

"No. I don't want to fly without you."

"Guapismo . . . it's only for two hours. I want to fly ahead. I need to make sure everything is perfect for you."

"I still don't know where you're taking me."

"Well, you're flying to Havana. There are direct flights now from Fort Lauderdale to Havana. Once you're there, I will meet you in a limousine and take you to our secret hideaway for the next five days. Then we'll come back here, spend the weekend with our family and we all fly back to Spain."

"I still don't want you to leave me."

"And I want to give you the best vacation ever."

I waved my hand around. "It already is."

"Not yet, tesoro . . . not yet. But very, very soon."

CHAPTER FOUR

I slept in Mio's arms all night but hated waking up without him. He'd left me another note, this one on his pillow, a red rose laid on top of it. It simply said I love you.

As I moved around packing my bag, George came to bring me coffee. I shouldn't have been hungry, but I was. The kids were upset that Mio had gone and were very unhappy to know I would be leaving them, too, but breakfast together was a wonderful distraction. I hated saying goodbye to the kids. Saying goodbye to Mama was just as bad. As I suspected, Papa drew me aside to give me some love advice before I left for the airport. Papa was my go-to guy on Spanish romance. He'd once instructed me on the mechanics of the Book and the Rose festival in Barcelona, a romantic day that is bigger than Valentine's Day.

I waited for his pearls of wisdom as Belen stood beside him to translate in English in case I needed it.

"Don't worry about anything," he said. "And bring me back some cigars."

"That's it?" I asked, stunned.

"What kind of advice is that?" Belen asked.

"Good advice." He looked affronted. "Primo and Violetta will cry, but I will take care of them. So don't worry. And don't forget my cigars." He patted my shoulder, which for Papa was about as emotional as he got.

Mama got hysterical, as did the kids. Belen walked me down to my waiting car service. "Thank you for loving my brother," she said, hugging me. "And don't worry. The children will be okay. I'll take them swimming, and we'll get some ice cream."

"I'll miss you," I said.

"I miss you already." She kissed my cheek, then ran back inside, but not before I'd seen the tears cascading down her cheeks. I got into the car feeling very torn. I'd gone weeks not seeing my parents . . . months now. I had no relationship with my sister. But Mio's family . . . it was a wrench not seeing them almost every day. Would I survive five whole days without them?

My cell phone rang. "Tesoro?"

I grinned. It was my Mio.

"Yes, it's me."

"Are you in the car?"

"Yes, and I'm on my way."

"Good. Because this was a very bad idea. Next time we play this game, you're coming with me."

I could practically see the frown on his face, which made me smile.

"Are you smiling?" he asked.

"Um . . . yes."

"You are a cruel man, Evans. See you soon."

I didn't know until the driver handed me my itinerary that I would be flying to Havana, a thirty-seven-minute clip from Fort Lauderdale and from there I would take a short, half-hour flight to the small island of Cayo Largo. I missed Mio already and realized this was the first time we had been apart since I had moved to Barcelona. I could pretend he was meeting somebody for coffee . . .

But that brought anxiety. Who was he meeting and why?

Boy, I had it bad for Mio.

I had come a long way, or so I thought. I'd become quite . . . accepting of the many, many friends Mio had. The truth was, he included me in everything, especially business, but occasionally it was fun for him to meet his friends and laugh about old times. Fun for him . . . but for me, agonizing. I shouldn't have felt threatened by his past, but I was aware I had an astonishingly handsome, magnetic man and that most of his friends desired him.

When I thought about all the times we'd hung out with Jaime and Marcus I wondered now, did Jaime secretly covet him? We arrived at the airport, and I trotted over to the Jet Blue counter. As I waited for help, I thought about Mio. I was glad he missed me. Very glad. He had booked me on the only weekly Jet Blue charter flight to Havana. It was a short flight, but my passport and driver's license were scrutinized by three different people. I had brought my small bag and wouldn't be checking it onto the plane. Naturally, at security they went through my cabin bag, then the passport and Barcelona ID again.

Mio had urged me to apply for Spanish citizenship, and after this routine, I began to see why. I had a valid California driver's license, but I lived in Spain. I began to fret that they thought me suspicious, especially when I went through the procedure once more before I reached the departure lounge.

That left me with a brief half-hour wait before I boarded the plane for the twelve-thirty flight. It was still a big deal for direct flights to be going from Fort Lauderdale-Hollywood International Airport into Cuba, apparently, because a live band arrived to play as we lined up to take our seats on the plane.

Since the thirty-year ban had been lifted just a few months ago, there was a definite spirit of excitement as we all boarded. I fretted that I'd do something goofy to get me yanked off the plane, then I worried that I'd brought no gifts for Mio. Up until now, it hadn't occurred to me, but now that I thought about it when we were lovers traveling from one city to another to meet, I'd always brought him something.

A love letter. I would bring him that. He adored love letters. I smiled to myself. I would write it as his client, his high-paying, smitten client. The idea tickled me. I opened my notebook to start writing and found a note from Mio.

"I have loaded a song on your iTunes. April Sun in Cuba."

That made me smile. When I'd accompanied him to one of his naughty sexual encounters in Italy, he'd downloaded Italian lessons onto my iPod. That seemed so long ago now . . .

As we ascended, I turned on my iPhone, slipped my earbuds in and listened to the song. I loved the tropical feel to the tune with its maracas, bird noises and catchy lyrics. Take me to the April sun . . . I replayed it several times as I scrawled him a letter. It occupied my every moment except for when I accepted some soda water from the attendant. I tore the pages I'd written from my notebook and folded them. I fashioned them into a bird. I thought it was appropriate since I'd been listening to the song. I almost wrote, Mio across the bird's beak, then remembered, he was Alejandro on this trip. My hot little man-whore.

He wasn't waiting for me, much as I'd secretly hoped, but a Cuban band was. It was hilarious. It was like stepping into a scene straight from I Love Lucy with Ricky in torn jeans and a big, tattered straw hat. I had to scramble to go through customs, catch my next flight via Aerogaviota. I made it to the second terminal with minutes to spare. The flight was fascinating as the small plane flew lower and I got to glimpse Cuba's gorgeous, white-sand beaches. I longed for Mio and wondered what the hell I would ever do without him.

I accepted the mimosa the flight attendant handed me, as well as the dried plantain chips. I wasn't particularly hungry . . . not for chips, anyway. I began to think about what I would do to Mio first the moment I got him naked and alone.

We were flying into Juan Vitalio Acuña airport. I had read enough biographies of Che Guevara to remember that Acuña had been a big support to him and the other political rebels of the 1950s. I didn't know much about his private life and wondered if he'd left behind a woman who'd pined for him when he went into hiding in Bolivia with Che. All in all, I knew I was damned lucky. I had a man who was loyal and loving and didn't go drinking and partying. Or getting himself shot to pieces.

I hoped. Oh, God . . . I missed him so much.

As we descended to the little coral island of Cayo Largo, I grinned at the stunning view. The tiny but modern-looking airport seemed set apart from the rest of the island, which, from what I could see was a few huge and beautiful resorts clustered around the shores of one edge. I couldn't wait to explore.

April Sun in Cuba danced in my head as we landed. I was totally stoked to discover the neat little airport had one runway and that we would walk to the terminal, a whitewashed building with a red roof. As we disembarked, I scanned the waiting throng of people waving madly at loved ones rushing into their arms.

No Mio.

I did get another mimosa and was treated to more music as I began to worry. Some people went off arm in arm, others went to the baggage carousel . . . and I . . . I stood and waited. Had I made a mistake? Was I in the wrong place? Just as I was about to call Mio, a man holding a sign saying McCoy arrived, looking harried. I rushed over to him.

"Ah, Señor McCoy! So sorry . . . I had a flat tire." His English was very good . . . more than anything, I was relieved he'd showed up.

"I am Eduardo. Señor Alejandro is waiting for you."

Alejandro. Was our cute little Cuban driver in on our game? He took my bag and ferried me to a small car curbside. I saw a few people from the plane including a lesbian couple posing for photos. The lesbian couple waved at me. I waved back. I climbed into the backseat of Eduardo's ancient 600 Fiat. I'd never seen one in person before. My dad, the car aficionado, had driven one of these rear-engine little beauties the year he'd lived in Florence and he'd never stopped talking about it. They'd stopped making them back in 1969, however. I was astounded that Eduardo was still able to find tires for his car.

"This is a classic," I ventured as Eduardo pulled away from the curb.

"No, Señor. My car is old. But she is all I can afford."

We drove down a clean-looking street toward the ocean. We were surrounded by ocean, actually. As we streaked away from the airport, I saw the entrances to some massive and impressive-looking resorts. I strained to get a look at everything around me. The water was aqua blue and the sand so white I could see straight to the bottom even from the car. It wasn't but a few minutes before we approached a huge resort called Sol Cayo Largo. It was magnificent. The gardens were lush, and I noticed a maze of swimming pools with lavish, tropical foliage, palm trees swaying in the breeze and, beyond these, the ocean stretching out in front of me. Eduardo parked haphazardly and turned off the engine. He opened my door, and I stepped out, the scent of wildflowers greeting me.

I felt Mio was close by. My body seemed hotwired to his. I was overwhelmed by the beauty of the place as Eduardo liberated my bag from the trunk. I followed him along a lush walkway, my head swiveling in every direction as we rounded a luxurious path toward a cluster of white-painted buildings to out left. Nope. It wasn't those. Closer to the beach, there were four large suites on two floors, overlooking the ocean. These seemed more secluded . . . and probably more expensive. He led me to a corner suite that had a Caribbean feel with a red roof, and from what I could glimpse from the open windows, colorful furnishings inside.

And then I saw him.

Mio was waiting for me. He wore a small, very tight black swimsuit. I recognized it as an ES Collection piece made by a Barcelona designer. It was one of my favorites and Mio knew it. I loved that small strip of fabric because it accentuated everything in front and in the back, well . . . the back displayed his luscious ass fully naked. All it had was the strip of elasticized fabric holding it together. He was magnificent, perched on the edge of the wooden railing of a balcony that overlooked the sea.

He was a sun god, and I was his mate, drawn to him . . . wanting him. Every second of that moment was precious, but my eyes focused only on his beautiful face.

I thanked Eduardo and took my bag from him. I tried to tip him, but he waved me off. Mio's gaze locked with mine. He never even glanced at Eduardo as he got off the little ledge and tilted his head, indicating he wanted me inside. I walked around the corner and saw a private area with white-painted wrought iron tables, tropical umbrellas with grass matting, and then I saw a trail of red roses on the ground. I trotted up the few steps to the door of our suite, a pair of crossed red roses on each one. I bent to pick them up. He wasn't at the door as I turned the handle and walked inside. The smell of roses was strong as I stepped across the polished hardwood floor.

And there he was, a single, gigantic red rose in his hands.

"How was your flight, Mr. Smith?"

Mr. Smith? Oh, yes, I was his happily married client who lusted after him.

"It would have been a lot better if you'd been on it with me. When I pay for your services, Alejandro, I pay for your company, but the roses are a nice touch."

He seemed surprised. Frankly, I surprised myself. I'd longed to hurl myself into his arms and slurp all over his cock. He grinned at me then.

"When we make plans to meet again, I will make certain to travel with you." His eyes held a gleam of mischief. "But it will cost you a lot more."

"And I'm willing to pay."

He grinned then. I thought he might laugh, but he didn't. Instead, he handed me the rose. "For you."

Inside the petals, I glimpsed a tiny gold key. "What's this for?" I extracted it and held it up to him.

"Fur-lined, golden handcuffs. If you can find them, you can use them. You can cuff me to the bed and do whatever you want to me."

I started looking.

"Mr. Smith." He moved over to me quickly, taking my face into his hands, "Aren't you going to kiss me?"

"My wife never wants me to kiss her."

"You can kiss me whenever you like."

Man, his cock looked so gorgeous wedged inside that tiny swimsuit. The only time he ever wore it was by the pool in our apartment complex when we booked it for a private, late-night swim. He knew I liked looking at him in it. Damn him. He was hot. I envied the man he had back home, then almost pinched myself . . . that man was me.

I stepped into his arms, and his kissed turned feral fast.

Slipping the gold handcuff key into my pocket I slid my hands to his ass, holding him tight as his mouth swarmed mine.

I loved his kisses, but I'd longed for his cock all day. I pulled away from him in spite of his protests.

"Are you always in such a hurry?"

"I'm famished," I argued as I knelt before him and kissed the crotch of his tiny black swimsuit. He smiled. "My wife . . . she starves me. Besides . . . she has nothing like this on the menu." I gripped the narrow strips of fabric at his sides and yanked. His cock sprang out at me.

My lover laughed. He was enjoying my ravenous pleasure. I tried to capture him with tongue only. He toyed with me, rubbing it back and forth across my face and lips. Occasionally he'd let me catch his sweet cock head, only to whip it away again. Soon, he was too worked up to torture me any longer. I had no idea if anyone could see in the bright, shiny windows and I sure as hell didn't care.

Mio's hands stroked the hair back from my face, and I sucked him, drawing my tongue over his cock head. He made a tsking sound. I knew this drove him crazy. I plunged my mouth back down taking him all in. He moaned loudly, biting off what I knew was going to be Evans. Instead, he ground out, Smith.

He came deep in my throat, his hips bucking back and forth as I struggled to swallow him.

When I came off him, wiping my mouth with the back of my hand, I couldn't resist. "You have someone special at home, Alejandro?"

"Yes."

"He's a lucky man."

Mio grabbed his semi-hard cock and ran it against my chin. He had a thing about running it against my stubble.

"No, I'm the lucky one." He smiled down at me. "You ready for your next surprise?"

I nodded eagerly, and he held his hand down to me. As I got up, I saw the array of multi-colored roses in pretty vases along the windowsill. Candles dotted the spaces between them. He'd arranged pillows and soft throws along a bay window overlooking the ocean.

He pulled up his swimsuit.

"We're going for a swim," he said. "I hope you brought something sexy to wear."

No, I hadn't. I hadn't even thought about it. I had board shorts in my ba, but they were the "guncle" kind. Back home we laughed about our gay uncle clothing.

He pressed his lips into a thin line. "Hmmmm . . . .just as I thought."

My cheeks flamed. I was a flop of a hot client. For sure. I hadn't thought about being sexy for him. I hung my head.

He came straight over to me. His hands reached for my face, tugging my chin towards him.

"I love you. Don't ever tell my boyfriend that. I never tell that to a client." He suddenly frowned. "Ever."

"Why am I an exception?"

He lifted his shoulders in that wonderful, yet maddening way of his. "I have left something for you on our bed."

Mio pointed to the bedroom on our left. I wanted a kiss. He must have known because he gave me one, before gently pushing me away from him.

In the bedroom, I was stunned to see that it was painted lilac. A little overwhelming at first, it was actually perfect. The decor was elegant, the four-poster bed, perfect.

I dropped to my knees and looked under it.

"What are you looking for, Mr. Smith?" Mio's feet were beside me.

"The handcuffs."

He chuckled. "You think I would leave them in such an obvious place?"

"I was kinda hoping." I rocked back on my heels. I was eye level with his cock. I kissed his stretchy swimsuit fabric.

"Hmmmm," he said. "Somebody in this room can't follow instructions." He yanked me to my knees, spun me around and pointed to the bed.

"This is what I want you to wear."

"What the hell is it?"

I picked up the tiny black and white-trimmed swimsuit that had a sizable anal dildo stitched into the back of it.

"I found this and thought it was perfect for you."

We rarely used toys, and I'd never seen anything like this. "Really?"

"Really. I will get you ready for it. We'll take a swim, and you will be stimulated the whole time."

"Oh." Now I was excited by the idea. "But I'm stimulated around you all the time."

"Not like this." He batted his eyelids at me.

I laughed. "Okay. I trust you."

He leaned in and kissed me.

"Get naked," he said. He began to unpack my things. I'd never seen this side of things, but liked the way he kept our things separate in the drawers. Not like us. Our things were always mixed together.

He turned as I slipped off my shoes and socks.

"You have a wonderful body. If you were my man I'd be all over you," he said.

"That's good to know." His mere gaze got my cock going boing.

He took me into his arms and kissed me, his lips making their way down my body. He gave my cock and balls a few tongue swipes, then flung my legs open, kneeling between them to feast on my ass. I almost came from excitement, but he stopped just in time. He leaned back and picked up the swimsuit. The fabric had looked shiny and soft when I first seen it, but it had a slightly stiff feel to it as Mio picked up my right foot and slid it into the leg opening. He pushed the swimsuit up one thigh.

"On your knees," he said. I did as I was told. He licked and sucked my ass as I swayed in front of him, expecting that massive butt plug to disappear inside me. He caressed and sucked my balls from his kneeling position and gripped my now raging cock and pulled it down between my legs. He gave it a cursory kiss, then some well-intentioned licks, then, from under one of the pillows, opened a small bottle. He leaned over my body, holding it to my nose.

"Coconuts," I said.

"Uh-huh." He smeared some of the cool lube onto my ass and began stroke me with gentle fingers. He leaned into me as one finger slid into my ass. He kissed me, dipping one, then two fingers into me. I got lost in his embrace, his hands working on my ass and cock, moving back and forth, arousing me in the places where he knew how to touch me. I was more than ready when I felt him sliding the swimsuit higher. I wondered how he was going to get the butt plug and the other leg of the swimsuit to fit when I heard him unclasping something.

I turned to look. The other side of the swimsuit's edge unlocked. I opened my mouth, but before I could say a word, he'd started working the butt plug inside me. It felt cold, hard and wet. It wasn't an uncomfortable feeling, just . . . strange. He began to pepper my back and ass with kisses as he fucked me with his new toy. Just as I was starting to like it, he slipped the rest of the swimsuit around my ass and locked it into place. He kissed my ass, stroking it.

"There," he said. "It stays nice and tight as long as I want it to. Now we go for a swim."

"We—what?" I didn't think I could walk around with that thing embedded inside me, but Mio had other ideas. He helped me off the bed, and suddenly the dildo inside me hit all the right places.

"I feel . . . funny," I said.

He grinned. "Funny?" He led me outside. I was starting to sweat. I'd never walked around with a dildo in me . . . and it felt weird until we ended up outside. He led me to the sand, where I stared into the clear, blue water. The dildo was working on my prostate and doing remarkable things to it. I dropped to my knees, and the feelings inside me exploded. I stared at the dozens of starfish lying on the bottom of the ocean floor—like gigantic gold stars—as Mio knelt beside me. He stroked my back and ass.

Sweat ran down my face as he spoke to me. I couldn't follow anything he said. I was too busy having the most intense orgasm of my life. He reached behind me, tapping my ass, shoving the butt plug a little bit higher. I panted as I came inside the snug, tight swimsuit, the sun beating down on me.

"Still feeling funny?" he asked. He led me by the hand into the water. I crawled like a dog, but I felt absolutely fantastic. I would have done anything he asked at that point. The dildo, still deeply wedged within me, was rubbing my prostate beyond pleasure to an itchiness I couldn't describe. I floated, face down, staring into the water. A million gold stars for me . . .

I awoke inside the lilac room, a concerned Mio staring down into my face.

"Are you okay?" he asked me. He sat beside me on the bed, a bowl of soup in his hands. It was still daylight, and he still wore his swimsuit. I reached down to my cock, relieved to find I was naked. No way could I have tolerated more of that dildo . . . even though my body still craved the force of my erotic eruption. My cock was hard.

"I sucked you to wake you up."

"Did I pass out?"

"Yes. Too much pleasure. I think I'm jealous of that thing.

I never made you come like that."

"But you were there. You did it."

He lifted his shoulders. "I guess. Would you like some soup?"

"Sure. It smells good. What is it?"

"Ajiaco. A Cuban specialty. Here . . . I feed you some." He spooned some into my waiting mouth.

"I love you," I said around the pungent mouthful of meat and vegetables.

"Me or the soup?" he asked.

"The soup." It was suddenly agonizing playing this game of forbidden romance, but deeply sexy too . . . like the butt plug. "Where's our toy?"

"It is having a little rest until our next vacation."

"We're having another one?"

His eyes bored into mine as he fed me more soup. "Of course we are. I think I like you, Mr. Smith."

"And you haven't even fucked me yet."

"That will soon be rectified."

He moved forward, putting the bowl on the bedside table. I took advantage of his actions to rub my hands on his spectacular ass. He turned, fire in his eyes, as I scrunched down and dropped kisses on his butt cheeks.

Mio made a tsking sound as he reached around to my back and stroked me.

"Mr. Smith . . . you are so persuasive."

He hadn't seen his hot new client in action yet. I swung him on the bed, positioning him onto his belly. Licking and kissing his crack, I played with the stretch fabric of the G-string he wore, shoving it aside with my tongue, then snapping it back again. He began to arch into me, wanting my full attention. I gave it to him. I sucked his ass for all I was worth. My hands moved under his taut belly to seek and find his beautiful, thick cock.

He grabbed me, repositioned us, and mounted me from behind. He fucked me fast, faster, his body drenched with my juices. I didn't know where his started and mine ended as he shot into me.

After he pulled out, his mouth clamped down on mine.

"Tasty," he whispered when we'd stopped shaking at last. He licked my lips.

"Me or the soup?" I asked, making him throw back his head and laugh.

CHAPTER FIVE

Mio — Alejandro wanted to take me to dinner, but I wanted to eat alone, naked in bed with him.

"Please indulge me," he said, an unhappy expression on his face. "I planned this whole evening."

"Okay," I said, but I was far from pleased. Didn't I, as his high-paying client, get any say in this?

He busied himself at the bar in our living room. I watched him mix something into a cocktail shaker and, with a secretive tilt to his smile, he dashed away. I could hear the bath taps running. It was evening, and we'd spent all afternoon fucking, my ass pleasantly sore. Even my lips were chapped from all our kissing.

"I will make you happy," he promised as he came back to me and kissed me again.

He'd never let me down in the joy department so I just lay on the sofa, a satisfied, happy man-puddle, smiling and wondering what he could possibly have planned that could top an already amazing, erotic afternoon. I gazed out of the window beside me at the lone, dimly lit boat bobbing in the ocean. Now those people had the right idea . . .

Mio returned, took my hand and led me into the bathroom. The tub was strewn with rose petals, and he'd poured something blue and ocean-smelling into the water. I let him wash my back as he climbed in behind me. I leaned into him, and he kissed my temple, his arms finding their way around me. We sat like this for a long time. I loved the feeling of his cock at my back, his arms, and legs surrounding my body. I kissed his left knee that bore a tiny scar I'd only noticed months after we'd been together. He'd sustained it at the age of seven, playing soccer at school. It was the only blemish on his body, and I loved it, always paying special attention to it.

He took his right arm from me and picked up the cocktail shaker I hadn't even noticed waiting for us by the tub. He poured the contents into two martini glasses and passed one to me. Rose petals clung to my skin as I turned around to look at him.

"What is it?" I asked as we toasted each other. The cocktail was dreamy. I tasted pineapple and rum and something else . . . sweet and tart and delicious.

"It's marrasquino, a Cuban cherry cordial." He smiled at me over the rim of his glass. "How is my happy-making campaign going?"

"Swimmingly," I said. "The water smells like the ocean and roses . . . and sex. I love it."

"We should bottle that scent." He leaned into me and kissed me. We polished off another glass each of his sinful cocktail, then he pointed me toward the bedroom. "I have your clothes laid out on the bed. Get ready, then I have something special for you."

Oh, boy! I raced to the bedroom and found a pair of the shortest, briefest sexiest board shorts I'd ever seen. I knew without even touching them that they were ES Collection. I slid them on. Man, I looked good!

I admired myself in the blue and black shorts in the mirror of our lilac bedroom, and then I heard a chuckle. I glanced over to see my darling in a pair of black and white shorts. Now, this was my kind of dinner attire! He held out his hand to me.

"Come." I naturally obeyed. We left our suite, the heady scent of tropical flowers heavy on the still-warm air. He held my hand, leading me to the beach where I was amazed to see the boat I'd noticed earlier, anchored not far from shore.

My lover bent, sweeping me up into his arms and charging into the ocean with me. Sea froth kissed my nose and toes. We laughed as we plunged in for the last few feet. We sank beneath the waves, rising in a kiss. We swam for the boat, scampering up the ladder our apparent skipper hoisted for us. I was giddy with pleasure when I glimpsed the table set for two inside the cabin.

Our host, Luis, showed us around the cozy digs. He was an attractive man, probably around forty, with dark hair, white cargo pants and loafers, a navy T-shirt and a killer body. The table was low, surrounded by huge cushions. I knelt beside my lover, who rubbed small circles on my back as I studied the magnificent table setting. Chocolate stars wrapped in gold paper, tiny starfish apparently made of peppermint flavored candy, tiny, edible red roses and, beside my glass was the note I'd written Mio on the plane.

Mio waited until our host poured us each a glass of champagne.

"Your first course will be ceviche, island-style," Luis said. "Bon appetite."

As he left us, I took in the rest of the room. Kerosene lamps and deceptively screened windows gave us privacy and a bug-proof venue where we could enjoy our meal in total privacy. I could hear music . . . Ah . . . April Sun in Cuba. It soon gave way to some Cuban guitar music. At least, I assumed it was Cuban.

Mio picked up his glass, as I did mine. He toasted me.

"You taught me the love of words . . . and language," he said. "I loved the letter you wrote me."

"I meant to give it to you." I shrugged . . ."I love you."

"And I love you."

We smiled at one another. He picked up what looked like a tiny, thin pancake, scooping some ceviche onto it with a little gold spoon.

"Which brings us to a problem," he said, squeezing a lime onto his little creation and popping it into my mouth. My whole body did the wave as I chewed on his offering. I could taste the freshness of the blend of raw fish. Marinated in lemon and lime, my lips puckered at the first tart note, then turned into a grin as an unexpected sweetness lingered on my tongue.

I was in love with this stuff.

Mio kept feeding me, and I him, until we were practically licking the cut-crystal bowl in which we'd been presented with our appetizer.

Luis returned to take the remnants of our first course, leaving us with a bottle of dry white wine, but we were still enjoying our champagne. We were hungry, and the smell of our main course flipped my lid. Luis presented us with fresh lobster, steak and white asparagus, which Mio fed to me with his fingertips the moment we were alone.

"You mentioned a problem," I said, remembering Mio's earlier comment.

"Si, Señor Smith. I have fallen in love with you, too. This means I can't have any other clients. You will be my only one."

"I see no problem here." Like a little kid, I stuck my finger in the dish of hot, buttery sauce and sucked it.

"On the contrary. It presents a big problem. If I am to service only you I have certain . . . requirements."

"Oh, really? Such as?"

"More letters. I really like those." His sidelong glance at me indicated some mild reproof. "It's been a while since I got one." He picked up the letter. "I like the shape you made it into. I like how you said I gave you freedom and love. Damn you, Evans, you make it so fucking hard to play this game."

"That's Señor Smith to you, pal, and I still don't see the problem."

"Can you stick to roleplaying?" he suddenly asked. "If we ran into people and were forced to converse, would you tell them I'm your husband or your hooker?"

"That depends."

"On what?" His eyes gleamed now.

"On how badly I want to shock them. So, your condition is that I stick to our agreed roles in public."

"Yes. I would like that."

"Anything else?"

"Yes. Don't let me forget Papa's cigars. He's already sent two text messages, and Primo misses us very badly." For one single, tiny moment, I saw the sorrow in his eyes. We loved those children.

"We need to find them a dog when we get home. Violetta wants one. We can assume all responsibility for him . . . or her. But no fancy pooch. I want a shelter dog. I—"

Mio slapped the table. "Roleplaying! We don't discuss family matters when we are roleplaying!"

"You brought up the cigars."

"I slipped."

He was too adorable. I leaned in and kissed him. "Have some asparagus," he said, dipping a spear into the butter sauce and holding it to my lips.

Luis came to take our plates and his lover, Andreas, rushed in to meet us. It turned out he was the chef. They ran a small but apparently successful business catering private events for gay couples.

"We'll be back before our vacation is over," Mio assured them. "I think we're ready for Señor Smith's special surprise."

Luis grinned. The two men left us with our final glass of champagne. I sank back into Mio's arms. Our swimsuits soon came off, and we were all over each other by the time our adorable hosts showed up with a large white platter bearing two gold boxes.

"What's in them?" I asked, very pleasantly buzzed, gripping Mio's rigid cock, which was barely concealed under our table.

"I don't know," Luis said. "We are dying of curiosity."

My gaze flew to Mio's face. "You're supposed to pick one," he said. "Whichever one you select will be the toy I fuck you with tonight."

I swallowed. "And the other one?"

"You will always wonder what might have been."

Damn him. I almost opened both but realized they came with tiny keys. Mio held them both. I picked the box on the right, and he unlocked it. Luis, Andreas and I all held our breaths as I opened it.

Nipple clamps. Gold nipple clamps. I wasn't into them at all . . . mind you I'd only ever tried them once.

"Oh . . ." Andreas looked ecstatic.

"Can we give the second box to our hosts?" I asked Mio. He narrowed his eyes and looked at me.

"Yes, provided they don't reveal what's in it."

"Really?" Andreas was off the hook with excitement.

They took the box and ran from the room.

"And now we go home for dessert and coffee," Mio said.

"Where is the key for the handcuffs?" I demanded.

He gave me a sly grin. "Where you left them, in the pocket of your jeans, but you'll never find the handcuffs, guapo."

"We'll see about that."

He hugged and kissed me, getting me beyond hard. I'd only just realized we'd been moving around the ocean and now we'd stopped.

"Time to go home," he said, picking up his swimsuit. Luis came to escort us ashore. I wondered where Andreas was and caught a glimpse of him hiding from us. He was lying on some cushions across the stern with a golden gag ball in his mouth.

Ah . . . that's what was inside Mio's second box. All in all, I felt I'd made the luckiest choice. We jumped from the boat's ladder into the water. It was cold and refreshing. We splashed our way to the sand and ran to our room.

In our suite, I was surprised to see that somebody had lit the candles surrounding the window sills and that there was a golden, domed plate in the middle of the coffee table.

I could also smell coffee. I wasn't sure I wanted it. If I was going to be having kinky sex I needed to keep my buzz on.

Mio, however, wanted me to enjoy a cup of Cuban coffee. He seemed so anxious for me to sample everything the island had to offer, and since he'd apparently planned everything down to the last detail, I accepted a cup. We sipped, sitting in our window seat, watching the waves and the stars meeting at the horizon.

"Are you happy?" he asked.

"I am very happy." I cast an apprehensive thought towards the nipple clamps. Would I still be feeling this way once I got those babies attached to me?

Mio began to kiss me.

"What is the strangest experience you ever had with a client?" I asked.

"Guapo, don't ask me about other men when I'm making love to you. For me, all other men are dead."

"Good," I said and meant it.

He took my cup from me and led me by the hand to the coffee table, where he picked up the domed plate from the coffee table. In our bedroom, he placed it in the middle of the bed and began to kiss me again. He stripped my shorts down and kicked his off as well. It was no surprise that both our cocks were hard.

Easing me onto the bed, he covered my body with his. He reached over to the dish on the bed. I wasn't sure what I was expecting, but it sure wasn't another bloody candle.

"Oh," I said, working hard to contain my disappointment.

He chuckled, moving the candle to the bedside table. He lit it, then picked up a remote control beside the bed. The fan overhead began to whir slowly, hypnotically. The candle began to flicker.

"I'm going to lick your cock in time to the candle. It's an old . . . well, it's a lovely custom my mother taught me."

That surprised me. "Mama taught you this?"

"Of course. She's a very bad girl. Just ask my father."

I clamped my hands to my ears. "Not listening."

He moved my hands away. "You must listen. This is a sexy game for you." He kissed me again, licking his way down my body.

I began to get into the mood he'd set, the candle, the cooling fan, shades of light, the smell of the wax . . . what was that smell? It was wonderful?

And then there was his tongue. It moved like liquid silver over my thighs and ball sac. He sucked me until I was practically delirious. He took advantage of my arousal to clip the nipple clamps into place. I jerked and writhed as he tongued around them. Sparks of intense heat flowed through me. He leaned down on me, kissing me, my leaking cock trapped between us. He slid a couple of fingers into me, moving his mouth back to my cock.

I stared up at the fan, the candlelight skittering like tiny flames across my closed eyelids. In spite of wanting to prolong all the good feelings, I started to come. Mio seemed ecstatic. He gripped my cock with his free hand, sucking, licking, swirling his tongue over my cock head. He took my entire length into his mouth. At the last moment, he tweaked the clamps, and a million little shards of starry light went off in my brain. Colors collided . . . condensed. My mouth hung open and, still, I almost stopped breathing.

"What is the scent of the candle?" I asked.

"Sex on the beach. You like?"

I nodded. Some people fall asleep counting sheep. I counted stars. Lots and lots of gold stars.

The next morning, one of the resort workers brought us breakfast in bed. She was a sweet woman, who lowered her eyes when she saw me naked in Mio's bed. Well, she must have realized I was naked. He wore a towel around his waist. She seemed very grateful for the Cuban pesos he slipped into her hand.

"I have something fun in mind for us today," he told me as soon as we were alone.

"Not sure I can stand much more fun. Mio, yesterday was incredible."

"Guapo . . . including today there are four more. I am so pleased it's going so well."

"What is the plan?" I asked him, as I picked up a piece of pineapple and munched it.

"We are renting a scooter. We are going to ride around the island . . . we need to get those cigars, and next, we'll go to a turtle farm. I know you love turtles."

I did. We romped through our fruit, eggs, and hot rolls, then showered and changed. In our shorts, T-shirts, and sneakers, we were typical tourists out to explore Cayo Largo. We stopped at the hotel's scooter store and rented a slightly battered yellow scooter. It took us thirty minutes to reach the front desk. I'd had no idea the day before that the place was so huge.

We ran into the lesbian couple I'd seen on the flight over. We introduced ourselves, then I introduced Katrina and Jenna to Mio. They were enraptured of course. Mio could charm the wings off a housefly.

"You broke the rule," he said to me as we got onto the bike outside.

"What rule was that?"

He turned and grinned at me. "You said I was your husband, not your whore."

"I made a decision. Split-second. They looked like they wanted to sit on your face."

"Yes, the blonde one did. You know I'm not interested in women. And if I'm to be your exclusive whore, you must play by the rules."

I frowned at him. "I think they might become friends of ours."

"Hmmm . . ."

He turned, started the engine, and we took off with a roar. The wind whipped our faces as we rode across the paved road. I soon learned it was the only paved road on the island. We drove down to the marina and to the turtle sanctuary. The man who ran it explained his problems with saving endangered sea turtles. Predators of all kinds stole the turtles' buried eggs before they hatched.

After showing us tons and tons of the beautiful creatures, he took us to the small lagoons filled with injured turtles he was rehabilitating. I was enthralled but beginning to get depressed. Though the suggested donation was a peso, we gave him twenty, and he would not stop hugging us.

Next door was the cigar shop the hotel concierge had recommended even though Sol Cayo Largo had a store of its own with a humidor and several popular brands of cigars.

Mio gave me a quick lesson in choosing the perfect cigar. Not being a smoker, I knew nothing about them and wondered how Mio had acquired his knowledge. Once again I felt like I was having an I Love Lucy moment . . . in the episode where she and Ricky go to Cuba, and she squashes his uncle's cigars and tries to replace them. Mio seemed perfectly relaxed with his choices. He bought a box of Cohiba Siglo VI for his father and a box of Romeo y Julieta Churchills for his uncle.

"Perfect," he said.

"We have to buy something for our women . . . and the children."

He looked at me. "That's true. We'll get them something at the hotel. There is a man who comes into the lobby in the evenings with a huge table selling arts and crafts."

"That sounds good. Have you bought things from him before?"

He narrowed his eyes. "No. Until you came along, I didn't buy anything for anyone. Now everything is presents! Presents! All the time."

I quirked a brow at him. "Really?"

"Really. When are you writing me another love letter?"

"Umm . . . today?"

That made him happy. "Now we have a quick look around the island, then I have something special for you back in our room."

"Oh, and what's that?"

"My cock."

We looked at each other and grinned. "I'd like to have that now."

He nodded. "Okay. You like the island?"

"I love the island, but I love you more."

"I should hope so. You've just met the island." He gave me a kiss, and we mounted the bike again. I held onto him with one hand and the cigar package with the other. All I could think about was having him. I kissed his back as we arrived at the hotel.

We deposited the bike at the rental shop and began the trek back to our suite.

He took my hand as we walked in the sun. "I booked dinner tonight, even though they normally don't take reservations, at the best restaurant on the island, Las Trinas, which just happens to be right here at the hotel.

"How convenient!'

"Isn't it?" He grinned. "I think we can handle spending a few hours fully clothed eating a wonderful meal."

"Fully clothed?"

He laughed. "You should see your face." He wrapped his arm around my neck and kissed my face and head. "We can be naked until then."

Goody!

Inside our suite, he wanted to take a shower. "Are you going to join me?" he asked.

"I think I'll get started on my next letter to you."

He pointed at me. "Five minutes, then I need you."

I picked up my notebook, which was on the bedside table. Normally, I scratched notes all day long, even in the middle of the night. I'd been so preoccupied with our hot holiday I hadn't written a word. I sat on our bed and thought a moment. The letter I'd written on the plane had been full of sex, innuendo and a client's passionate devotion to his high-paid escort.

Alejandro,

Since the moment I met you, I knew you were different. You approached me at the bar in the hotel in London, and I did something I have never done before. I went to bed with a stranger. I felt so bad when we said goodbye and realized I had feelings for you that didn't make sense when I hardly knew you.

I had no idea who you were and what you did. I know you realized that and I am certain it's what gave us a chance. You told me today you never gave gifts until I came along, but it's not true. I knew you as a kind and generous man from the first moment your hand touched my skin. I know other men paid for the privilege of your attentiveness and I try not to feel jealous.

In my own way, I try to make up for the life you lost, the planning, the detail that went into all your assignments. I have always feared I am not enough. No. I know we are meant to be together and that you don't miss those days. Therefore, I gratefully accept being your only client, and I promise to stick to the rules.

I love this forbidden liaison of ours, and now I know why you didn't take presents home from your business trips. It was because you have always kept business and family separate. I am touched and honored to be part of your family.

I chewed the end of my pen a moment.

"Guapo, where are you?" he called out.

"I'm coming," I called back. Not quite. But I would be. And suddenly I knew where he'd hidden his golden handcuffs. Oh, he was smart, my man. I bounced off the bed and looked for the pants I'd worn the first day. They were lying on the back of a chair, and I rifled the pocket for the key.

Turning to our closet, I opened the doors.

"Guapo!"

"Coming!"

His suitcase was on top of mine. He'd carefully unpacked both, and he knew I wouldn't even look in my bag, but when I opened it, there they were. They were beauties. I grinned as he called for me again. I stuffed the luggage back in the closet, closed the doors, popped the cuffs under our bed with the key, and hastily stripped.

He pouted at me from the open shower door until I was in his arms under the stream of cool water.

"What took you so long?"

"I was writing you a love letter."

"Yes, I know. Did you need so long to think?"

I kissed him, which effectively got him to quit grumbling. We took our time soaping one another, kissing the clean spots, chasing suds away with our tongue.

"They taste like sex," I said against his mouth.

"We are sex." He turned off the taps, led me out of the shower and picked up a fluffy towel. We dried off and went to our bed. I pushed him onto it, making him laugh.

"So bossy today."

"Oh, yes. And I'm in charge."

He leaned up and looked at me. "You think?"

"Yes. You said if I found the cuffs, I'd be in charge."

He looked stunned. "You found them?"

"Of course I did. You hid them in my suitcase. I have no idea how long they've been there."

"Not long. I kept moving them. I never thought you'd look in there, though."

"Because you know me so well and I wouldn't want to think about losing my April Sun in Cuba. But you know what? You're my April Sun."

He opened his mouth, and I kissed him, claiming him for my own. He didn't resist when I cuffed him to the bedposts.

"And we are not going to any fancy restaurant," I said as I hunted for the butt plug swimsuit. "Where is it?"

"I'm re-thinking the rules of this game for the next trip," he said, but he was smiling.

He directed me to the bottom drawer of the bureau. There were a few toys we hadn't played with yet, and I couldn't wait. I brought out the butt plug and joined him on the bed. It was a joy to suck and lick his cock unobstructed . . . not that he ever stopped me from sucking him, but I wanted to take my time. I didn't use the nipple clamps on him. I'd do that later. He humped my face as my lips closed in on his balls. I tugged gently on them, making him moan.

I dipped down to his ass and licked it. He jumped at my tongue-touch. I sucked and stroked at his hole, and his legs opened wider. I rarely got to fuck him, but I was a man on a mission. He went crazy when I finally let him suck the plug.

"We haven't had a threesome since we were in Italy," I told him. He glanced up at me. "This is the only way we'll ever have one. I am going to call our new friend Jimmy."

He sucked on Jimmy, and I took him away from Mio again, who gasped.

"I'm seeing a side of you I never saw before."

"Alejandro, you've seen it. You brought it out of me." I grabbed the coconut-flavored lube and worked some into his butt and some onto Jimmy. I slowly fucked him with it, Mio's ass gobbling it up. His cock was reaching, straining for attention. He let out a yell when I shoved Jimmy all the way into him.

I licked his glistening cock head and smeared a little lube on my ass.

"Oh, God," he ground out. "Get on me. Now!"

I climbed onto his majestic cock, taking pleasure in his need, his desire for me. I fucked myself slowly onto him as his mouth fastened onto my right nipple. I cradled his head in my hands. I soon lost all control. I could feel the strain of his tethered hands, his marauding cock buried deep inside me.

We came together, Jimmy fueling Mio's deep-burnt orgasm. He raised his face for a kiss as I came all over him. On us. The smell of sex. Stars. And a man who'd awakened me and all my senses.

And brought me to life.

YOU MAY ALSO ENJOY THE FOLLOWING FROM EXTASY BOOKS INC:

The Book and The Rose
A.J. Llewellyn

Excerpt

"So . . . Evans . . . is it okay if I call you Evans?"

It's my name, dumbass. "Sure."

"I know you had a really great run and some hot numbers with Out of Step." He took a deep breath.

Oh, here we go.

"So tell me, how is Nora doing? Is it true she's in a lockdown facility?"

In the four weeks since he'd been actively hunting for a new job, Evans had been able to sift interviewers into two categories. Those genuinely interested in maybe giving him work, and those who wanted fresh Nora North gossip.

"She's in rehab and doing great, but as I am sure you're aware, her health comes first, and the network decided to pull the plug on the show. After all, she is . . . was the show."

Mitch swung in his chair. "Right, right. So tell me, is there any truth to the rumor that she took off her clothes and went running through the Paramount lot begging strange guys to fuck her?"

Shit! How much does he know? She even begged me and I'm gay!

"No. Absolutely not."

Mitch kept asking questions. Evans moved Mitch into Category B, bit down on his disappointment and bantered, feigning interest, allowing his mind to wander. He could drift and dream . . . alone on his own mental private island with Mio-Alejo Cortez, the hot Spanish businessman he'd had not just one, but two scorching encounters with. Just the thought of that man's sensuous mouth on his body made him squirm in his seat.

God, I want to call him, but I have to play it cool.

Evans still couldn't believe his luck meeting Mio on that brief trip to London. He'd never seen a man who oozed so much sex appeal. His dark, silky hair had been cropped short, but still managed to look dreamy with his widow's peak and thick, dark brows. He didn't smile much, but when he did, he was electrifying. His English had been limited when they met in the bar at the Dorchester. The second time he'd run into Mio, the man had whipped out a Spanish-English dictionary.

He'd smooth out a piece of paper on which he'd written, *I crave to speak to you.* That paper was still in his wallet. It carried Evans through some tough times dealing with his bleak moments in the Hollywood minefield.

"You are more than handsome," Mio had said. "You are beautiful."

They'd spent the afternoon and evening in bed. *Lips, eyes, mouth, tongue, teeth . . . there wasn't a part of him I didn't like . . . or spend hours lingering over.*

A late supper and a night of unhurried, but passionate, nonstop sex had ruined Evans for any of the studio idiots he met back in Los Angeles.

"You know, I met her once at a party up on Summit," Mitch was saying when Evans tuned back to the present.

Evans knew where this conversation was heading and

didn't want to take this road at all. Just saying Summit was an industry catchword. It meant that Mitch partied — hard — and wanted to know if Evans did. Or if Evans knew about those big pool-and-sex parties up on luxurious but decadent Summit Drive.

"I know nothing about her . . . partying," Evans said. "Look, she's a friend. A friend I care deeply about. I wish her the best. I'm sure you do, too."

She fucking killed my career and my show. A show that took me six years to get into production. Right now, I fucking hate her.

"Right, right. You're right." Mitch pointed a finger at him. "She was hittin' the snort pretty hard though and . . ."

He allowed Mitch to ramble on. Evans wanted to think about Mio. Mio, who'd called him from Spain three weeks ago saying he had a business trip to Miami.

"Meet me," he'd implored. "My hands . . . they need to touch you. My mind . . . it needs you. You are my tesoro."

His treasure? Evans would have flown anywhere, on his own dime to see him, but having another man value him enough to fly him out first-class for a hot weekend had been alluring. They'd met at the airport . . . oh, what pleasure it had been to see Mio in his trademark Saville Row suit and hand-sewn Turnbull and Asser shirt.

Their chemistry had been undeniable . . . even more intense. They both knew their first fling had been no fluke.

He hadn't bothered Mio with much of the drama of getting Nora into lockdown, the surgery she required after destroying her septum, the cartilage between her nostrils, due to snorting so much coke. Losing the show. He'd been so delighted with the respite, the adoring attention of his handsome, debonair lover. He smiled, thinking of Mio's childlike glee in buying Chicken McNuggets, dipping them in honey and feeding them in bed to Evans . . .

Now he'd been back two weeks and two days. Each day without Mio got worse. They talked at least once a day and the calls became shorter and shorter. It hurt them both to talk . . . and also, not to talk. Evans felt tears pricking the back of his eyes. Mio had been a beautiful dream that both harmed and helped him. In some moments, he could imagine a future with him. In other moments, the slender, invisible thread between them seemed to snap.

"So what are you working on now?" Mitch asked.

Evans jerked back to reality. "I've been wanting to meet with you about doing a new series with Heliconia."

"Right, right . . ."

It galled that Out of Step had been his entire creation and now it was locked in contract hell with the network. He couldn't use the name or recast the lead. He had to start again.

"The thing of it is that we're not looking to get involved in television right now."

Evans remembered that last afternoon with Mio. They'd gone for a swim at the hotel pool. Mio had run into a couple of guys he knew and introduced them to Evans. They'd been such good-looking men, but before the conversation could start, Mio whisked Evans back to their room.

He was amazing. Tender . . . passionate . . . funny. I'll never meet anyone like him ever again. But our lives are separate. Ha. You might even say out of step. I need to be here, and he's as European as olive oil.

Evans smiled at Mitch. "You approached me about your new vampire series. We were supposed to —"

"Vampires are passé now, Evans. Fantastic name by the way. It's your mom's last name, right?"

"Yes."

Why did you bring me here if vampires are on the slide?

He contemplated asking the question out loud. He had nothing to lose except his health benefits, but Mitch answered it for him.

"Zombies are where it's at. Zombies are the new vampires."

"Absolutely," Evans said. "Which is what I wanted to talk to you about."

I can switch my pitch to zombies . . . but I thought they were hot two years ago.

"We already have two zombie shows slated. Two movies . . . if they fly, I'd like to talk to you about running a series for us."

Fuck! That could take another year . . .

"In the meantime, I was wondering . . . I don't have a job I can give you, but I thought . . . you know . . . maybe we could have dinner one night . . . soon?"

Mio's body . . . hard, smooth, skin the color of caramel . . . yet he couldn't keep his mouth off mine.

"No," he said. "I'm involved."

"Oh . . ." That threw Mitch. He was used to being the guy in charge, clearly. "That's weird . . . only I asked around, and word on the vine is that you're single."

"I don't . . ." Evans took a breath. "I'm pretty private, Mitch." He stood. "Thanks for the meeting. I really appreciate your time."

Mitch scrambled out of his chair. "Oh . . . well, thank you. Uh . . . have a nice day."

Evans shook his hand and looked him in the eye. "You have a nice day, too, Mitch." You jerk.

He walked out of the office, past Silvia's desk. She didn't glance up at him, and he knew she'd listened to the whole thing. She didn't look up because the business meeting had gone badly and her boss's clumsy attempt at getting a date had flopped.

This was the latest in technological progress. Studio executives bugged their offices during meetings so that pesky writers couldn't claim they'd stolen ideas after pitch meetings, which they routinely did.

"Thank you, Silvia," he said, mindful of being polite and friendly with her. Today's personal assistant could be tomorrow's studio boss.

She glanced up, smiled and also wished him a nice day.

Yeah, nice. He stood outside and checked his cell phone for messages. He longed for a call, just one little text from Mio. He remembered their last moments, Mio between his legs, fucking him, his mouth clamped over Evans'.

I never wanted to leave him.

He called his agent, Kelly King, who took his call immediately.

"How did it go?"

"A bust. He wanted a date."

"I hope you said yes."

He laughed.

"Are you going over to visit Nora?" she asked.

"Yeah."

"Well, you'll need a drink after that. It's on me. I'll meet you over at Residuals. Let's say one?"

"Are you kidding me? I don't start that early."

"Oh, excuse me." He loved Kelly. She always made him laugh. "How's five o'clock?"

"Sounds good to me."

He ended the call, got into his six-month-old Prius and thought about calling his assistant, Michael, who was hanging by a thread emotionally and financially. Evans helped the guy out with bills and with constant pep talks. When the show was canceled, he'd promised Michael he'd find them a job, he'd take him with him. Nora North's drug addiction had not just wrecked his show, she'd demolished the hopes of the wonderful crew Evans had fought hard to assemble.

Now it looked like she had ruined his career. He was being punished for her sins in Hollywood.

I'm all washed up, and I'm only thirty-two.

Evans pushed out of the parking lot and hit a red light. It was a long one. He sat, not wanting to listen to music or talk radio. All he wanted was Mio's smile. To hear his laugh one more time. The sun sparkled, and it should have heartened him after long weeks of unprecedented rain. Except that high above him overlooking Riverside Drive, the poster of perky, pretty Nora North promoting Out of Step, a poster that had been there for months was being covered up.

He watched the workmen with long-handled sticks pasting up the long, single sheets that would make one gigantic poster.

A part of him wanted to step on the gas and go straight out into the intersection and let the other, unsuspecting drivers kill him. A part of him wanted to . . . no, needed to stay alive in case Mio called.

His cell phone rang, and he plugged it into his dashboard circuit.

"Hello," he said.

"Hola, Evans."

The light turned green, and a car honked him from behind.

It was him. It was Mio.

ABOUT THE AUTHOR

A.J. Llewellyn lives in California, but dreams of living in Hawaii. Frequent trips to all the islands, bags of Kona coffee in her fridge and a healthy collection of Hawaiian records keep this writer refueled. A.J. loves male/male erotica and has a passion for all animals—especially the dog, the cat, and the turtle. A.J. believes that love is a song best sung out loud.

To find out more about A. J., visit www.ajllewellyn.com, or you can email her at AJ@AJLlewellyn.com.